The Things We Cannot Change

A STORY ABOUT THE GHOSTS CREATED BY ADDICTION

ALLISON SPOONER

Praise for Allison Spooner's Work

"Spooner's writing is effortless, weaving and worldbuilding while readers enjoy the ride. Thoughtfully paced, *The Lost Girl: A Neverland Story* is buoyed by strong craft."

BookLife Prize

"Equal parts poignant and nostalgic, and full of adventure. The Lost Girl is

a beautiful reminder that growing up isn't so bad."
– Andrew J Brandt, Bestselling Author
of Picture Unavailable

"Ms. Spooner expertly constructs her narratives like tiramisu, alternating layers of striking detail and delicate subtlety. She moves with ease from un-natural to upbeat to unsettling to up-lifting from beat to beat..."
Amazon Review of Flash in The Dark: A Collection of Short Stories

"I don't know if I've ever found an au-thor that is able to capture emotion in it's most visceral and raw form the way Allison does."
Amazon Review of The Problem With Humans: And Other Stories

A Note From The Author

This story is truth and fiction rolled into one. It depicts my real experiences and complicated feelings of living with and losing my father to alcoholism. The story may be fiction, but many of the scenes are pulled directly from my life. In this book, I set out to tell the truth, which may be hard for many to hear at times, especially those who have also experienced life with an alcoholic. While I hope this book can help many face complicated emotions and begin to heal from old wounds (like it did for me), I understand that reliving those experiences may be difficult. If it's too difficult at any time, I will understand. This book and my story will be here for you when you are ready.

This book is dedicated to those haunted by the ghosts of addiction.

"We cannot hide from our ghosts. Whether they are real or not. We must make peace with them."

A Haunting in Venice (motion picture)

Chapter One

The pain from the past came haunting,

knocking at my soul . . .

E.S.

The two-story white house winks its green shutters at me, welcoming me home as though it's missed me as much as I've missed it. I smile as I approach the house set back on the inside of a rounded corner, a large oak placed perfectly between the front and side yards. There is a tire swing hanging from a tree in its lush and colorful garden and a Japanese cherry blossom that blooms magnificent purples and pinks for one month out of the year. A breeze kisses my cheeks.

Everything is perfect . . . except one thing.

My dead dad is standing in the driveway.

The house behind him, the house that was as much a place of comfort as it was a place of uncertainty, calls to me. It's inviting me to come play, come rest. Swing on the tire swing and read a book under the bright and blossoming tree and soak up the gentle spring sun. I want to accept its invitation. I want everything it has to offer me.

Except the dead person. I could do without him.

He's standing there, blocking my path home, his arms slightly lifted as though he's waiting for me to run in for a hug.

Maybe he thinks I'll smile, run toward him, and let him wrap his arms around me and tell him how much I've missed him.

But I don't.

The sight of my dead father waiting for me in front of my childhood home does not bring me joy or fill me with the urge to sit and chat about all the things he's missed since he's been gone. The presence of this man with jet-black hair slicked back and loose strands blowing in the soft spring breeze does not calm me. It terrifies me.

When a smile stretches across his stubble-spotted cheeks, I do not feel relief. I do not want to smile back.

I want to run. I want to go home.

But he is standing in front of that home, keeping me from it, keeping me from the peace I am seeking.

And that pisses me off.

I decide if I can't go into the house, I'll leave.

But I can't turn. I can't lift my feet. My breath comes faster and I feel panic squeeze my heart. I look up to find him staring at me, waiting for me to say something.

I look away.

Maybe if I ignore him he will fade away, just as he'd been fading away my entire childhood. Slowly deteriorating, wasting away to almost nothing.

But he doesn't fade. He doesn't move. He just stands, watching me, trying to make eye contact as I desperately try to avoid his gaze. My heart

is pounding in my throat, and I feel like I'm running, an invisible foe chasing me, even though I am
standing still.

He says my name and I jump. I shake my head,
trying to block out the sound, and his face falls. His
arms drop to his sides, no longer awaiting their
hug, and the smile stutters on his face.

My stomach twists as I see his shoulders droop
with the truth: his own daughter doesn't want him
here.

He says my name again, a pleading whisper that
echoes on the breeze.

And then, I wake up.

***

*Listen to a performance
piece inspired by this
chapter.*

I sit up in bed, a gasp and a sob fighting for dominance of my throat. Tears or sweat drip down my cheeks, I'm never really sure which.

I had it again. The dream where my dead dad comes back to life, and instead of being happy about it, I'm furious.

I hate the dream, and I hate him for making me have it. He's been dead for almost a year. Can't he just leave me alone?

It's a good thing my roommate has already gone home for spring break, because a groan escapes my tight chest as I swing my legs over the edge of the bed.

I'm so sick of this.

I push my damp blankets away from my body and glance out the window. The soft glow of early morning sunlight is peeking through the blinds, dancing across my pillow and beckoning me to lie back down, to let the cool pillowcase soothe my burning cheeks, but I don't. I can't. I know it will be a useless attempt. I haven't slept properly in months.

I stand and try to brush off the remains of the dream, but every night it stays with me longer and longer, like a doorbell that keeps clanging through a house long after the button has been released.

And as I get ready to head back to my childhood home for the first time in who knows how long, I know it's going to be even harder to shake.

I'm so tired. Tired of fighting this ridiculous metaphor every single night and tired of trying to shove it away every single morning. I'm not Freud, but I don't need my Psych 101 professor to tell me I have some pretty deep, messed-up feelings toward my alcoholic father, who died almost exactly a year ago. I've done everything I can think of to shake those feelings. I left my childhood town as soon as I graduated, which was only a few months after he died. I immersed myself in college life; I piled on the class load, joined clubs, and took on extra shifts at my coffee shop job. I didn't even have pictures of my family up around my room like the roommate who had left immediately after her last class on Friday to join her perfect family for some fun in the sun and bonding time. She talked to her mom every day on the phone, so I wasn't sure how she had time to miss her, but she did. She told me all the time.

And I miss my family, of course I do. But they remind me of him, and when I think about him, well . . . I was doing my best to leave the past in the past so why couldn't it just stay there?

The phone jangles from across the room and I jump.

There's only one person that calls the dorm's landline and I debate answering. I love my mom, I really do, and I like talking to her. I just know exactly what she's going to say, and I'm still half in the dream and sweaty yet chilled, and I'm going to see her soon anyway.

But I roll out of bed and stumble to the phone.

"Yeah, Ma." It's not a question, I know what she's calling about, and my brain is already trying to fight through the fog of my nightmare to find an excuse, any excuse, to get me out of what she's going to insist on, what I've already promised.

"You're still there?"

"I just got up. It's like *eight o'clock*."

"But you're coming?"

"Yes, I am all set to spend an exotic spring break in the exciting, rural, bustling—"

"Okay, okay. I get it. You'd rather be going somewhere more exciting, but you haven't been home in—"

"I know how long it's been." And I know I told her I would come, but . . .

I also know that once I'm home the things lurking in my subconscious will barrel their way to the surface, and there will be no shaking off dark dreams even in the cool light of day. "Look, I was actually thinking—"

"You *said* you took time off work and that you would get all your assignments turned in."

I swallow hard at the mention of my assignments and avoid glancing at the paper sitting on top of my desk. "I did but I—"

"Callie. You *need* to come home."

What I needed was some strong ibuprofen and a week of nightmare-free sleep. Something I would definitely *not* find at home.

"There was some stuff in my writing class." I don't want to tell her anything about the conversation I'd had with my creative writing professor or the red marks scribbled across my last story or the ultimatum he'd given me, but if it would give me the chance to spend a week alone in my dorm, wandering a quiet campus instead of spending a week in my childhood room haunted by memories, maybe it was worth it. But I don't get the chance to confess.

"I'm not arguing anymore. You're coming home. I'll tell you more when you're back, but I need you here. Do you understand?"

My mom rarely gets cross and rarely raises her voice, so her tone catches me off guard and I clench my jaw.

"Yeah, okay." There's silence on the other end and I can't stand it, so I fill it. "I guess my MTV spring break will just have to wait."

"Well, thank you for your consideration." Her tone has softened. "Call me when you leave?"

"No, Ma. I'll leave here shortly and see you at home."

"Okay, drive carefully."

"I will. See you soon."

I hang up, and sigh. I could have signed up for extra shifts since everyone was gone. I could have volunteered to help the few organizations that stay running over breaks for kids that don't go home. But for some reason, my mom has been insisting I come home for spring break. She's asked why I never come home before this, sighed that she never sees me anymore, but so far hasn't pushed the guilt . . . until now.

I stand up. My stuff is already packed and ready to go, and there's nothing stopping me from getting on the road for the hour or so drive.

I change into jeans and a sweatshirt, grab my phone charger, my favorite stuffed animal, and some books, shoving them into my backpack. Finally, I grab the paper off my desk. I don't mean to, but I look at it one more time. They use red so you can't ignore it, right?

"Devoid of feeling" is scribbled across the top, and if it hadn't been true, I might have cringed. But I've spent the last year shoving down my feelings and avoiding them, at least the bad ones. But my professor wasn't hearing it. It was my third "rough" story (that was what he called it because he didn't want to call any of our writing bad) and he was determined to get through to me, at least for the sake of my grade.

"You know," he'd told me, handing me the red-slashed paper, "sometimes putting pieces of our own life into our writing can help unlock something."

What did he want me to say? That I'm haunted by dreams where my dead dad comes back to life and those dreams are more like nightmares because when he died we *thought* we escaped sleep-less nights listening to him crying and begging for his bottle while my mom climbed into bed with me, her small daughter, her only comfort? We *thought* we left behind hours spent listening to him get sick and years of watching him wither away. Should I include that every time I am sucked into the dream I am terrified we only *thought* we escaped the stench of sweat and smoke, small-town talk, vom-iting, slurred frustrations, and incoherent rants? Should I write about how my biggest fear is that he'll come back with his demons and his bottles; that we'll have to go through it all again? When he died, he took a lot with him, but he left peace behind, and the idea of him teasing us with that and then taking it away pisses me off. Nobody wanted to hear *that*.

"This is supposed to be fiction," I told him. It's why I'd taken the class in the first place. Well, be-sides the fact that it was part of my creative writ-ing curriculum. It was also the class I'd been most excited to take. Unlike my poetry class, where you could just tell each piece was dripping with real tears and peppered with actual heartbreak and breakups and . . . *truth*—in fiction you got to lie. Make up lives, make up endings.

"Yes," he responded, "but even fiction has to *feel* real. It's still about life and life is hard. Haven't you ever been through anything hard?"

I took that moment to excuse myself and promised I'd do better on my final piece.

"Well, you have to," he'd said before I could yank the door open. "Or you'll fail."

My stomach had dropped. *Fail?* Me? Fail a writing class?

Writing was the only thing I was good at. It was the one thing I'd always had. When I'd struggled my way through math and science, I'd had writing. When nothing in the world made sense, I'd used writing to make sense of it. My English teachers loved me, I'd won the best portfolio award my senior year, I wrote a novel in middle school and another in high school. I won writing contests. I was going to *be* a writer. I couldn't *fail* writing. If I couldn't write, who was I?

And now I was going to have to work on my final piece at home, my mom hovering and my brother always . . . around. Without telling my mom I was failing, I couldn't get her to see why I needed to stay, and there was no way I was telling her I was failing. I'd tell her if asked directly, of course—I'd never been good at lying to her. Hiding my feelings, sure, but not lying. If she asked, I would squeal, and if she found out, she would be convinced something was wrong. Maybe she would try to get me to stay home and take classes close by, or worse, see a therapist.

I shove the paper in my bag and continue getting ready. I have a week to figure it out. I can lock myself in my room and get some writing done, no big deal.

If I could just get some sleep . . .

In the bathroom my roommate and I share with two other girls in an adjoining suite, I brush my teeth and wash my face. I swipe a little foundation under my eyes in an attempt to hide the dark circles and avoid concerned questions. The shade had matched my olive skin tone when I'd bought it, but lately I had the pallor of the cadavers I saw in the forensic science book I'd browsed when I'd briefly considered becoming a forensic scientist (before I quickly realized I'd rather write about dead bodies than look at them). I have to spend a few extra minutes rubbing in the makeup to avoid a two-toned mask. There is nothing I can do about the puffy eyelids trying to slip down over my dark brown eyes. They are desperate to close and it's all I can do to keep them open.

When I'm done, I can still see the dark circles under my eyes, and the skin around them is still a little swollen from what I assume was a middle-of-the-night sob-sesh. I never remember it, but every morning my face and sleep-deprived eyes remind me that my nights are no longer for sleep, they are for fighting my past.

Did they make makeup specially designed to cover up anger traced with guilt? Did they have tones that would hide the sheen of sweat that always appeared on my forehead when I woke up and re-alized I was the kind of daughter that would shun her dead dad if she ever got the opportunity to talk to him again? What kind of person is that? What kind of daughter doesn't want her dead dad to reappear for an emotional reunion after a year of separation?

This daughter. Hence, the guilt.

I shake my head. I don't think they have a foun-dation for that. This will have to do.

I am throwing all my toiletries into my bag when my phone rings again.

I almost don't answer it, but I've never been the type of person who can deliberately ignore my mom's calls.

"I'm leaving right now," I say, throwing my bag over my shoulder.

"That's great, but I'm just calling to see if you can make a quick stop on the way home."

Chapter Two

I must fight for my survival, or die be-

fore I'm old.

E.S.

I slam my car into park at the bottom of the long, sloped driveway and look up the hill to the white farmhouse with the slanted porch that wraps halfway around the house, partially obscured by a receding morning mist and as faded in color as it is from my memory. My breath shakes through my chest as I take in its peeling paint and the dilapidated, no-longer-red barn, set back off the property. The barn we used to explore despite the warnings about its shaky foundation and unstable structure. It was falling apart even back then, but that was part of the fun, the mystery, and the danger. In that barn you could see a whole history, and we'd tried to picture our ancestors, strangers with the faces of my dad or grandpa, baling hay or milking cows.

I can almost hear the teeth-chattering bark of my grandparents' jet-black Doberman and feel the anxious clench in my stomach at the thought of walking past his lithe body yanking against his chain, his tartar-stained teeth bared. He wasn't the family dog. He wasn't sweet or friendly like my childhood German shepherd. He was a guard dog. He lived outside and rarely had contact with people. He was well-trained, but he was not pleasant, and I often had dreams when I was little where our lovable, and also black, family dog would turn into the Doberman while playing and attack me. I've hated Dobermans ever since. There's no dog here today, and for that I am grateful.

I've always hated coming here, but my mom's request wasn't unreasonable, and I hadn't been able to think of an excuse that would get me out of the errand.

"The new owner of your grandparents' old house called and said she found a box that we should have. I told her I'd swing by and get it, but I just haven't had a chance. It's only a few minutes out of your way."

She was right and "I don't want to" hadn't seemed like the right thing to say at the time.

But on the drive over, as I'd gripped the wheel and dreaded stepping onto the property where we'd said goodbye to my dad, the old white farm-house suddenly seemed like the perfect solution to all my problems, and I kicked myself for not thinking of it before.

I'm done fighting with these dreams and my past. At eighteen I should be sleep deprived from too much partying or late-night study sessions, or from trying not to fail my writing class, not because of insane dreams about my dead dad.

But this old white farmhouse, a house I haven't thought about in over a year, is now right in front of me and I know what I need to do.

I know that if I'm going to end this, if I'm going to say what I need to say and end the sleepless nights and guilt-ridden visits with my dad, it has to be here. I can't go back to my childhood home with this ghost following me. The memories will only get more vivid when I cross into town and step into that house. I need to end this today.

There's no headstone where I can lay flowers or kick at the dirt. When my father was cremated, his ashes were spread here, on the farm where he'd grown up. I suspect his memories of childhood had been as convoluted as mine are of him, but I also know he'd been happy, once, somewhere. Maybe this was that place. I wouldn't know. I'd never asked.

Pushing open the car door, I leave the small Honda at the bottom of the hill rather than pulling up the driveway and parking next to the house, hoping the new owner won't notice I'm here until I'm ready to be noticed.

On the other side of the driveway, across from the house, is a field. Years ago it may have been lush with soybeans or maybe even corn, but today it's overgrown with weeds and dotted with the occasional crooked fence post. It's perfect.

I push farther into the field so I am hidden from the house, plant my feet in the damp dirt, and look around me.

What now?

My hasty plan suddenly doesn't seem like much of a plan.

There's so much I need to say, so much I never get the chance to say in my dreams, because I'm too shocked, angry, and confused to form words. But nothing is coming to mind now as I stand in an almost picturesque setting on a beautiful spring morning.

It would be better if it were raining.

I kick at the grass under my feet, dew soaking the toes of my white tennis shoes. A whisper escapes my throat. "Why?"

It's the question that's plagued me since I first heard the word "drunk" and it's the first thing that slips out now. "Why couldn't you just *stop?*"

He'd had so many reasons to stay sober: an incredible musical talent that took him to the cusp of stardom, a family that loved him, kids—kids who he scared the shit out of when he came home stumbling and yelling, kids who wanted to know him better, who wanted *him* home. Weren't those good enough reasons? Shouldn't his family have meant more to him than some bottle? But, no. He always went back. There would be months at a time when he would be fine and we would all be happy . . . but the drink always won.

I turn in circles in the middle of the field, dizzy with the memories of a deep, Elvis-like voice crooning from the edge of my bed, peaceful nights punctured by the sounds of his newly broken sobriety, my mom shoving us out the door as he screamed and begged her to tell him where his bottle was, a hand puppet peeking around the door during bath time, funny facts about old movies, the smell of whiskey mixed with sweat and cigarette smoke.

He was always there, but not.

He was my dad, but he wasn't.

And I hated him for it. I hated him for all of it, but I never got to tell him, to have a heart-to-heart or explore our relationship or my feelings, because instead of getting better, instead of fighting for his family . . . he'd died and left me with all this anger.

A groan escapes from the hard knot in the center of my chest. I'm not debating this anymore. It's time.

"Where are you!?" I call, lifting my face to the sky, to him, to wherever he might be. "I have so much I need to say!"

I need to release this. All of this. This anger, this grief, this burden he left when he died. But I don't think I anticipated how hard it would be to yell at an empty field. My mouth opens and closes and it's like the words, whatever I thought I was going to say, are stuck in my throat. He's not here. I can't say what I need to say to weeds. I don't know why I thought this place would hold some sort of imprint, a memory of him that I could face and . . . what? Yell at?

I look around me, searching for any sign that he was once here, that he can hear me or feel me or—

I gasp. My mouth opens again, but instead of releasing the burdens that have lived on my shoulders over the last year, I scream, step backward, and fall onto the damp ground, landing on my ass.

A figure stands in front of me where only moments ago there was empty space.

"What the—!?"

"I'm here, Callie. I'm listening."

I whip my head around, searching the surrounding field for a possible source of the voice coming through the morning fog—any source other than the shimmering figure still materializing in front of me. But there's no one else here.

This isn't happening. This is my nightmare brought to life, literally.

I fought the ghost of my dead father regularly in my dreams, dreams that felt so real it was hard to tell if I was crazy or just battling some really strong demons . . . or both. But this is different. I am awake. I have to be. I'd already woken up, gotten out of bed, talked to my mom, stomped my way here. There's no way I'm still dreaming.

But if I'm awake, how do I explain the figure standing in front of me? The thin, lanky man only a few inches taller than me, with jet-black hair, pale skin, and hazel eyes. The man I'd last seen in a casket.

This is real life, not the dream that's haunted me for the last year. This is the world where my dad died almost a year ago after slowly drinking himself to death. It's not the one where he comes back—and instead of being relieved, I'm mad. I don't want him back, I want him to stay gone. Night after night I have to watch his face fall as he realizes the cold truth: his daughter is glad he's dead. Both worlds suck, to be honest. But at least in the dream I wake up.

Right now, at this moment, I am not waking up.

He is standing in front of me, more solid than he was only moments before, and he is not disappearing and I am not waking up. Why can't I wake up?

He looks around for a moment, as though he's as confused as me (which is most definitely not possible). He takes in his surroundings, his curious eyes flashing with recognition as he sees the house and the field, and then settles his gaze back on me.

"Oh, Cal." He says it as though he knows exactly what is happening, sympathy dripping from his voice as he steps toward where I'm still sitting on the ground.

"Nope," I say, putting a hand out and scooting backward in the dirt, as if that would stop him if he, it, whatever, really wanted to get to me. "Nope. Nope." I say it over and over as though it's the magic word that will make him disappear again.

Am I going crazy? Has the last year of constant frustration, the realization that I am glad my dad is dead and the agonizing torment that comes with that realization slowly driven me insane so that my most haunted dreams, the ones I dread every night, have slipped into my waking moments?

Or is this, impossibly, real?

And which would be worse?

I've never believed in ghosts, but I've never not believed in them either. When my friends had séances at sleepovers, I was always the brave one. I'd go check the noises after every scary movie and lead the way in haunted houses, my friends gripping my elbows and using me as a human shield. Ghosts and ghouls didn't scare me. But my dead dad coming back, the possibility that after escaping years and years of watching him drink away every hope any of us had for a normal life, that scares the shit out of me.

"What is happening?" I mumble, rolling farther from the figure and onto my knees.

"I'm not sure," he replies, as though we're chatting over coffee, pondering a traffic jam or strange weather.

I shake my head and stand up. I'd come here for something, but *this* was not it. Brushing the dirt and mud off my pants, I move toward my car, giving the now completely solid figure a wide berth.

The sun is getting stronger as the day shifts into late morning, and my sweatshirt is suddenly stifling as I move quickly down the driveway, my keys already in my hand. As I pass the porch of the house I hear another voice, this time female. I'm afraid to look. I don't stop moving but glance over my shoulder and see a woman waving from the porch. The new owner of the house.

Shit. I almost forgot the whole reason I came here in the first place.

"Hi! Callie is it?"

Ignoring the fact that everything in me wants to run, I stop as I watch her lean down and pick up a box.

"I have something for you!" She hurries down the steps and closes the distance between us quickly.

She's a small, thin woman with a big smile and a lot of blond hair. She's probably around my mom's age, and she's happier than anyone I've ever seen living in this house, but when she stops in front of me, her bright blue eyes darken for just a moment. For a fraction of a second, her pink full lips form a small circle and she lets out the tiniest of gasps as her eyes dart toward the field.

I swear I hear her whisper, "Oh," before she re-covers her composure and pulls her lips back into a welcoming smile. "Oh, I'm so happy you came by. I found this the other day and your mom told me to call if I ever found anything that belonged to your family, so I did and—"

I reach out and grab the sides of the box. "Thanks." I'm trying to hurry her along, trying to escape whatever it was I saw in that field.

"I didn't look through it obviously, but I think it was your . . ." She looks down at the box she's still holding onto and then back toward the field. "Well, you should have it."

"Thank you," I say again, trying to shift the weight from her hands to mine.

She looks up at me. Are those tears in her eyes? Who *is* this woman? "It's just . . . I'm so sorry." She studies my face. "You're so young." She takes in my dark circles, and her eyes narrow as her gaze settles on my wide eyes that are darting from the field, to the box, to my car, and then back to the field. "Are you okay, Callie? Oh goodness, what a silly question. Of course you're . . . What I mean is . . ." She looks back to the field, following my gaze, and then leans toward me and lowers her voice, "Is everything all right?"

"Yes," I say quickly. "I'm just in a hurry. Thank you for the things."

"Oh, of course." She doesn't ask why I was making a beeline for my car before I'd even had a chance to get the box I'd come here for, but as she studies me, the dirt on my jeans, my hastily parked car, and my body half turned away from her, it's like she's piecing together what may have happened. But there's no way she can know. She hasn't let go of the box yet when her eyes meet mine again, and this time she doesn't look away.

"Facing the past isn't easy, but sometimes it's exactly what we need to do in order to let go. If we avoid it too long, it will find us. Have you noticed that?"

What is she, a fortune cookie?

"I . . ."

"Don't run from it, Callie. You'll do more damage than good."

I'm sure I must be staring at her like she's from another planet, but after her proclamation she simply smiles and lets go of the box. I stumble backward.

"You take care, okay? I'm always around if you ever need . . ." She looks behind me again. "Well, anything."

What could I possibly need from this stranger?

"And I'll stay out of y'all's hair this weekend, I promise."

I get my bearings, gripping the box before it slips to the ground, taking me with it, and by the time I can process what she's said, she's back up on the porch pulling the front door open.

Maybe she misspoke, I think, as I shove the box onto the floor of the back seat and hop into the front.

My heart is still pounding as I throw the car into reverse and back out of the driveway, gravel flying out from under the tires, leaving the past where it belongs and vowing to never force a confrontation with it *ever* again.

Chapter Three

*Now the war is raging inside me, on the
outside too . . .*

E.S.

I pull into the town I escaped as soon as my graduation cap left my hand. Well, mentally escaped, at least.

Physically, I had to spend the last few months of my senior year, and the summer that followed, going through the motions of a teenager who had just lost her father. Luckily, I was able to coast through the final weeks of school, and since he probably wouldn't have been able to attend my graduation even if he were alive, his presence wasn't missed—at least not by me. I spent the next few weeks finishing my shifts at my job in town, doing the summer reading recommended by my professors, and avoiding conversation around anything that didn't have to do with school, moving, or my new life.

As soon as my room on campus was available, I left. I packed very little from my childhood bedroom—just clothes and some books I enjoyed picking up over and over—and I leapt headfirst into my new beginning.

That was when the nightmares started.

While they started at school, they seemed to get worse every time I attempted to make a trip home. So, I didn't. Since leaving, I've been back as little as possible. Even over my long Christmas break I only came home to celebrate the day and immediately went back to campus, claiming I had work to do.

If I don't face the past, eventually it will fade away . . . right?

I turn onto my block and everything is familiar. The houses I've grown up biking past, the street I took to walk to my elementary school, and then my house, nestled on its plot on the curved corner of two quiet streets.

Okay, this is normal. This is what I saw every day when I came home from school or a friend's or a football game. But this is also what I see in my dreams. Dreams that taunt me with comforting details from a turbulent past before ripping that comfort and peace out from under me with the appearance of his ghost.

But I'm sure *this* isn't a dream. I'm sure my mom insisted I come home for the week, probably to all be together at the one-year anniversary of his death.

As I pull into the driveway, I am one hundred percent certain the house in front of me is real.

I know the cracked concrete that presses against my feet as I exit my vehicle is real, and the breeze blowing the leaves of the giant oak in the side yard is real, and I've almost convinced myself that the figure in the field was a temporary hallucination—until I see him waiting for me on the sidewalk leading up to the side entrance of the house.

Then dreams become mixed with reality, and I don't know where I am or what to do, so I freeze; one hand still on my car door as though I might hop back in, turn around, and never come back. Tempting.

I don't move and neither does he. We are at a standstill and he waits, his arms slightly lifted away from his sides like he's ready for a hug, just like the dream.

And just like in my dream, I don't move.

But unlike that nightmare, where the situation is just bizarre and sad and I know it isn't real and I spend only the next few seconds grappling with all my infuriating emotions and waiting to wake up, this time I am frozen in fear. Because I am still fairly certain this is real life, and in real life, people don't come back from the dead. In real life, ghosts are not real (or at least that's what I tell myself).

In real life, my dead dad only haunts me in my dreams. Until now.

So what the hell is this? I push the car door shut. I can't stand in the driveway forever, so I move around the car toward the house, avoiding eye contact with whoever or whatever this is while still trying to take in the details of the figure. He's steady, I notice. He doesn't sway or stumble, and when I risk a glance at his eyes, they are simply green with flecks of gold and even a little bit of the brown of my own, completely clear and unclouded, focused on me.

Okay, this is obviously *not* my father. At least it's not the man I knew most of my life.

Is this some look–alike stranger? Is this a preda-tor? Should I scream? My brother has been bigger than me since I was four and he was two, and he's tall and strong, but strong enough to take down a grown man?

Maybe *this* grown man, because he's as scrawny as my dad always was, even when he was off the booze and his potbelly started to come back. He's not much taller than I am now, five foot five-ish compared to my five three. Taylor could take him. We didn't always get along, but he'd protect his sister, I'm sure of it.

I stop walking halfway up the walk, afraid to get any closer. We stare at each other, an emotional game of chicken. He stands impossibly still like he's afraid I'll bolt if he makes any sudden movements. And I will. I don't want any part of this scenario playing out in front of me. Because this war of emotion raging inside me is so much worse than in my dreams. Yes, there's anger and fear but the guilt . . . oh, the guilt. Because once again I'm the daughter who doesn't want a second chance with her dead dad. I mean, I have missed him. Parts of him. He was my father, and despite everything, I did love him. I loved him, but after he died, I *never* wished he would come back. And there is no single part of me that wants to run to him now. This emotional roller coaster is his fault, and he must be able to tell because he shoves his hands into his pockets, folding into himself but keeping his gaze locked on me. Maybe he didn't mean to, but he destroyed any ounce of love or joy I should be feeling toward him at this moment. And for that, I can't forgive him.

So, I decide to do what I do in the dream. Ignore him. Push toward the house. Just like my dream self, I find myself hoping he will simply fade away as I move past. I am dizzy with the similarities, no longer sure of what's real. But just like in the dream, he doesn't disappear as I slip by. I keep walking, silently hoping the next part of the dream doesn't manifest here.

Please don't say it, please don't say it.

But the moment I am past him, he says my name.

I shake my head, ignoring him. Because that's what I always did when he stood on shaky feet trying to connect with his only daughter through glassy eyes and a haze of whiskey; I ignored him.

I hear my name again and flinch.

This is where I usually wake up, sobbing and soaked, my head pounding from the pain of the past that was knocking at my soul. I don't know what to do now, so I keep walking. I walk up the sidewalk. I leave the figure behind me, hopefully to fade away, and I open the door.

I step through the side door, through the sitting room that was once a record room when he was alive and is now a reading room for my mom, complete with a comfortable loveseat, built-in shelves lined with books and knickknacks and collectibles acquired over the years. I don't stop to see if he's come in behind me. I don't want to know.

I hurry through the house. It's a Monday, so my mom and brother are at their respective schools, my mom teaching and my brother probably struggling to make it to the end of the year. I managed to put off my homecoming until today and had a quiet weekend in my dorm, attempting to sleep in and lose myself in work, pushing my return home off as long as possible.

I bound up the stairs to the room that is thankfully still *my* room, even though I spend very little time in it these days. It's straight ahead, the last room at the end of the hallway at the top of the stairs; my brother's room to my right, a spare room to my left, and the bathroom just beyond that.

I push through the door. Someday my mom might change it into a sewing room or another spare bedroom, but for now it's still mine. It's still peaceful and comforting despite the years I spent hiding under the covers, trying to drown out the shouting or waiting for the sober shoe to drop.

As I step into the room, there is a flash of yellow at my feet and I gasp before realizing it's just Stormy, our aging cat. We've had Stormy since I was about six, which makes her twelve years old, but despite her advanced age, she's just as spry, adventurous, and sassy as she always was.

I lean down to scratch her head as she winds her way between my legs, her fluffy tail leaving yellow hair on the ankles of my jeans.

"Hi, Stormy."

She meows a greeting and then bounds farther into my bedroom.

It's clear a child was put in charge of naming her. She's bright yellow with flecks of white throughout her thick fur, but I insisted on the name Stormy, and as much as my mom tried to insist it didn't exactly fit, the name stuck.

I pull the door shut behind us, no idea if it will actually stop whatever may or may not be following me, and throw myself on my bed, trying to block out the morning's events.

It's still early so maybe I can get back to sleep. Stormy hops up onto the bed and walks across my legs, my stomach, my chest, as she tries to find the perfect place to settle.

I haven't been back in this bedroom, with its dark blue wallpaper and tan carpet, or in this bed, for a few months, not since Christmas. I haven't studied these walls, my books, my posters of favorite shows and teen heartthrobs that didn't make the cut when deciding what type of person I wanted to be before I left for school. The stuffed animals that didn't get to make the trip stare back at me mournfully.

I shove myself under the covers, annoying Stormy in the process, pulling up the comforter I got a few years ago when I redecorated my bedroom and got rid of the disastrous waterbed I thought would be cool but never actually had a heater that worked (so, in fact, it was *too* cool). The comforter that had taken me through the last few years of high school, that was there when I'd woken up to the news, that I'd been snuggled deep down under when I awoke to someone gently shaking my shoulder. Yawning, I'd sat up and found my mom perched on the edge of the bed. Blinking sleep away, I met her heavy gaze. Her eyes were bloodshot—the swollen, red-rimmed eyes of someone who'd been up much too long.

Before my brain could register that something was wrong, my gut was telling me exactly what it was.

"Daddy didn't make it," my mom whispered.

Unbidden, unwelcome, and zipping ahead of the hot tears that would soon fill my eyes, a single word beat out every other thought . . . *Finally.*

And that was the first thought I had when I found out my dad died.

Like your heartbeat thumps against your chest unnoticed and unacknowledged every second of every day, that word bumped against my grief as I'd moved through the motions of the days leading up to goodbye.

As I made my way down the stairs, knowing I wouldn't find him passed out on the couch, smelling like whiskey and bad decisions, pretending there wasn't an almost empty bottle of whiskey hidden in the cushions beneath him, the word echoed in my head with each step. *Finally.*

As the house filled with family members and the phone rattled with condolences, the chair just outside my parents' bedroom, where he so often sat and smoked when he was too weak from withdrawals to make it to the back porch, sat empty. Every time I walked by it, the word blended with the murmurs of adults making plans they didn't think I should be a part of. *Finally.*

As I curled up on the couch, my eyes glued to a country music marathon, I realized I would never again have to hear his once beautiful voice strained and cracked from years of smoke and abuse as he tried to recapture the talent of many lifetimes before. The word played in my head like a song. *Finally.*

As I gripped my grandmother's hand and played with her shiny, diamond bracelet in the pew of the church where he'd sung so many times, his voice came over the sound system. It was clear, the voice of his youth, of his life before the grip of addiction squeezed the talent and promise out of him. Tears filled my eyes as I wondered if his voice finally sounded like that again. *Finally.*

I didn't hear much as the minister spoke of his kindness, his talent, and his devotion to God. But when he came to the end of his speech, his voice softened. He looked at my family and spoke the words we'd all been praying to hear, "At long last . . . he is at peace."

I sigh, blinking away the memories.

He might have been at peace, a relief to so many that knew and loved him, but where did that leave us?

Stormy is still pacing and her paws press into my belly. She doesn't snuggle down next to me or plop between my legs like normal. She is sniffing the air, glancing around the room like she is watching a speck of dust only she can see. She lets out a questioning yowl.

"Stormy, lie down!"

I snuggle farther down into the covers, pulling the blankets over my head to block out the sun streaming in through the two windows in my room. I squeeze my eyes shut and try to empty my mind of all the memories, trying to release the anger making my heart pound. I try to forget there might be a ghost or a spirit or a hallucination wandering through the house I'd actually always wanted to be haunted. I let out a long, deep breath and feel the muscles on my face loosen. It's not a ghost, I tell myself. It's the product of too many sleepless nights. The vision at the farm was simply the product of stress and insomnia. Stormy jumps down to the floor and I relax deeper into the bed. A couple hours of sleep will help. When I wake up, he'll be gone.

Well, at least the figure following me around will be gone; his memory is steeped into these walls, this town . . .

I'm somewhere in the in-between land of sleep and wakefulness when I feel the bed next to me sink slightly under someone's weight. Stormy?

Or had I gone downstairs to tell my dad I couldn't sleep? Had I begged for a song or a back scratch to help me drift off even though I hadn't really been trying all that long?

I let out a small sigh as a gentle voice drifts into my consciousness. "Puff the magic dragon, lived by the sea . . ."

There's no guitar tonight. Just his hand on my back and a voice that is clear, steady, smooth. But it's a voice I haven't heard in years. It's *too* steady.

My eyes pop open.

I'm not a child.

I'm back in my bedroom during a visit home from school and he . . . he's there on the edge of my bed.

When I jump, sitting up and scooching back toward the wall at the same time, he moves away. He doesn't force proximity, but any proximity is too much when just his presence here is impossible.

"Hey, Cal. It's okay."

I shake my head. Absolutely not. This is absolutely not okay.

"How . . . ? Why?" It's all I can stutter out. This vision, or whatever it is, was not supposed to follow me inside. It was supposed to stay at the farm, or outside, or in the past, where I'd left it. Anywhere but right here in front of me.

I guess this is what I get for trying to face my demons—a total psychotic break.

What's going to happen to me? Will they lock me up? Will they try to perform an exorcism? No, that was only if you were possessed. Who did I know that could communicate with the dead? Wait, *could I?*

I don't want to know, but I have to know. Is this just a vision or . . .

"Can . . . can you *hear* me?"

He smiles. "Of course."

Of course? What does that mean? It's not the answer I want. I shake my head and pull the blankets back up, diving under like I'm trying to hide from the monster under the bed.

"This isn't happening," I mumble. Except I don't even know what is happening.

"Callie?"

I freeze. It's a different voice. Not his. My brother's. My brother who is probably standing in my doorway staring as I cower on my bed, shoved into the corner of the room with a blanket over my head.

I peek out from under the comforter.

"What are you *doing?*"

Such a brotherly response. Doesn't even think to ask if I'm okay.

"I . . . I thought I saw a bat." This would not be unusual. Our old house had winged visitors frequently in the spring and summer. It would be a plausible story if it wasn't—

"It's daytime."

"Well, duh. I mean, I could have scared it awake if it was sleeping in here. But I think it was just a dream anyway. What do you want? Did you even knock?"

"I tried, but you didn't answer and I heard you talking so . . ."

"Do you notice anything . . . *weird* about my room?"

He leans through the doorway, his blue eyes darting quickly around the room, and then shakes his head. "No."

"You didn't even look!"

But it doesn't matter. If he could see the figure standing in the center of the room, a smirk playing at the corner of his lips as he watches his kids bicker, I'm sure he would mention it.

"I looked enough. No bats. Nothing weird—just you."

I sigh. "What do you want anyway?"

"Ma—" he starts, and then stops, glancing into the room again.

My heart stutters. Does he see something? Is there a chance I am not alone in my craziness?

"What's up with Stormy?"

I turn toward where he's pointing. The cat is winding her way through the legs of the figure. To me, she is a traitor, welcoming her old friend back into her life and greeting him warmly. To an outsider's eye, to someone who can't see the apparition in my bedroom, it looks like she is walking in circles, stepping around absolutely nothing, staring up at empty air.

"Uhhh, I don't know. She's a cat. Cats are nuts."

Taylor shrugs. "Ma's gonna be home soon. She called and wanted me to make sure you were going to be here."

"Home? What time is it?"

"It's after three."

Three? I'd slept for hours.

I'd caught up on the sleep I'd been missing, and I was still having a complete mental breakdown. Perfect.

"Well, I'm here. Obviously."

He rolls his eyes and backs out of the doorway. "Cool."

"Hey," I call before he can go.

He stops.

"Do you know why she wanted me home so bad?"

He opens his mouth but then hesitates. "She wants to talk to you. She'll tell you."

"Tell me what? What's going on?" There is a slight tremor in my voice, and Taylor hears it, sensing my panic.

"Everything's okay, just . . . She'll be home in a few and will fill you in. You should get out of bed." He rolls his eyes again before turning back around, heading down the short hallway, and then bounding down the stairs.

I'm left with a lingering feeling of dread and a ghost in my room.

I risk a glance at *him*, wondering if he knows what's going on. Are ghosts omniscient? Could he see what was happening in the rest of the house while I was sleeping?

He shrugs as if sensing my question. Of course he wouldn't know and I immediately curse myself for engaging with a ghost.

A ghost. Am I already starting to accept that I'm being haunted? It seems more likely than a hallucination . . . doesn't it? It's certainly the more welcome of the two . . . *isn't it?*

"Callie! I'm home, are you here?"

Taylor must have told her I was, but she needs to check anyway.

"Yeah, Ma! Be down in a sec."

"I'm making some sandwiches. Do you want one?"

"Sure!"

I sigh and pull myself out of bed. I've been sleeping in the sweatshirt and loose jeans I put on this morning, but I don't bother changing. I run a hand through my chin-length bob, and when I see it standing up in spots, I grab a beanie from my backpack and pull it on. It's still cool enough for beanies and probably will be for another couple of months. Unless you traveled south, you didn't get an actual *spring* break in Michigan. You just got a break. And it seemed I couldn't even catch one of those.

I ignore the figure and my traitor of a feline and head downstairs. If he is a ghost, maybe he'll go away when he realizes I don't have anything to say to him.

I skip down our enclosed staircase, counting the steps under my feet. Twelve behind the wall, the thirteenth is the landing that opens up into the living room when you take a slight left, and the final steps go down into a long room lit by a huge picture window overlooking our quiet street. The TV is to the right and the couch is just under the window, but no one is waiting there today.

I move through the large room, split into two sections by a loveseat facing the TV and two different area rugs covering hardwood floors. The front door opens up into the second half of the room, a sitting room with two chairs and a decorative table behind the loveseat. My parents' bedroom is off this room, and before you can get to the kitchen, you move through a smaller room that houses a piano and French doors to the backyard. The flow of the house is strange, I'll admit that. But it's old. It was built in the early 1800s, originally just one level and a few rooms, and was slowly and a bit haphazardly added onto over the years. And even though I some-times complained about its age and its moans and groans, I secretly loved this old place.

My mom is at the kitchen counter and glances over her shoulder when she hears me come in. You couldn't sneak around in this ancient, creaky house.

"Well, good morning." She turns and leans against the counter, crossing her arms. She knows what time it is.

"Hi, Ma."

The sun from the window bounces off her short light brown hair, hair that was once the same shade as mine but has lightened after years in the sun and some boxes of hair dye. She keeps it cut close to her head and her face is round and kind.

"You came."

"You called."

"Hasn't seemed to matter before . . . but I'm glad you're here anyway." She turns back to her sandwiches.

"So what's going on?" I ask, sitting down at the dining table set off to the side in a small nook lined with windows. The house didn't have what you would call flow, but it definitely had its charms.

"I can't just want you to come home?"

"Just seemed pretty . . . urgent. Is everything okay?"

"Yes, everything is fine. We're going to have a memorial."

I swallow. "A memorial?"

"Yes. For your dad."

I assumed that much. "But . . . why?" I didn't mean to sound callous or insensitive but . . . *why?*

"To mark the one-year anniversary. It's Saturday."

This Saturday? "But . . . we had a funeral." I didn't want to be argumentative, but I guess I just didn't see the point. We'd put all that behind us. Movement near the doorway catches my eye, and I turn to see Stormy prancing into the room and just behind her—

I put a hand over my mouth to stifle a gasp or a groan, I'm not really sure which would come out at this point. Well, we'd *tried* to put it behind us.

He waltzes into the kitchen like he has every right to be here, like he still lives here and is just coming in to grab a snack or make one of those disgusting frozen White Castle burgers he always loved. I try to motion toward the door with my eyes, tilting my head toward the exit, urging him to beat it. But he just smiles when he sees us and does not take the hint.

My mom turns, a sandwich on a plate, and walks over to the table. I turn my attention back to her. She narrows her eyes, but if she notices my pantomiming, she doesn't acknowledge it. "Sometimes we're not ready to say goodbye so close to someone's passing. Especially when that passing is sudden or our feelings toward them are complicated."

Complicated was a kind word. Probably something she'd gotten from an Al Anon meeting. But my feelings weren't complicated and his passing certainly wasn't sudden.

Sure, I'd been surprised, shocked even, when my mom woke me up that day with the news. It was a surprise in the moment, but my dad had been walking around for years looking like death warmed over, already a ghost haunting his family and creating more and more unfinished business.

I didn't see the point, but I could tell it was important to her, so I could show up, nod and smile, and then go back to school and get back to forgetting . . . well, attempting to forget.

"Okay," I say, taking the plate. "Thanks."

"And I'd like you to speak."

I swallow my bite of sandwich whole and my eyes start to water as I squeak out, "What? Why?"

"Like I said . . . sometimes we're not ready to say—"

"I said goodbye, I don't need to do it again." My tone is harsher than I mean it to be, but nothing in me wants to do this. I don't want to gather with family again, I don't want to talk about him and his life, and I certainly don't want to be the one speaking about . . . about *what?*

"You're good with words, Cal," she says, ignoring my snippy response and heading back to the counter. "Always have been."

My stomach clenches as I think about the red marks on the paper shoved into my backpack upstairs.

I sigh, not sure it's fair that just because I can string together a sentence, I'm the one being forced to put together a hokey speech filled with platitudes I don't believe.

"This is kind of short notice. You couldn't have called and told me?"

She lifts her eyebrows and I already know all her answers.

"You always say you work best under a little pressure."

"True, but . . ."

"And the more notice I gave, the longer you'd have to back out."

"I . . ." It's true.

"It doesn't have to be a novel, Cal. I have full faith in you."

She starts cleaning the counter, keeping her hands busy like always, and I sneak a glance at him. He is watching her like he's never seen her before. Like he's never noticed the way she moves or her purposeful actions. I wonder how long it's been since he'd had a clear, sober view of his family. Stormy is sitting next to him.

"I'm going to need your help the next few days, to get everything ready," says my mom.

I haven't said I'll speak, but it sounds like she's not waiting for my assent.

"It's at the farm," she adds.

"Of course it is."

"And you'll say a few words." Again, not a question.

"I really don't think I—"

"Please, Callie. This is important."

Out of fear of sounding like a three-year-old, I don't ask why again.

"I know you think he's gone and it's over and we should move on. But that's also easier said than done."

I don't tell her that maybe he isn't as gone as we think. "It's not that. I can't . . ."

She stops what she's doing and turns to face me, waiting. She is willing to hear whatever it is I have to say. Frankly, she's probably been waiting for me to open up for months. I feel him watching from the doorway, as attentive as she is. But I've always been taught that if you don't have anything nice to say about someone, you shouldn't say anything at all . . . and that's exactly why I don't want to say anything at the memorial. But this moment, with both of them staring at me, doesn't seem like the *right* moment to point that out.

"Okay. Fine."

She nods. Before turning back to her cleaning she glances at Stormy.

"What are *you* waiting for?"

Stormy just meows.

My mom looks at me and I shrug. She continues with her list.

"His friend Chuck has a few guitars of his and he wants us to have them back. And then Manny has some music of his. I thought you and your brother could pick out a song or two to play at the memorial."

"In the middle of a field?"

She glances over her shoulder and looks at me out of the top of her eyes, not a fan of the sarcasm. "You don't have a player that takes batteries?"

"Okay, yeah."

"So you can pick that stuff up?"

"Taylor can't do it? He knew his music friends better."

"He has school and practices and homework. Your spring break doesn't line up with ours, but I took off a few days later in the week to take care of some other stuff. He'll help you with the music."

"Okay, sure."

"And you got that box from the farm?"

"Oh. Yeah. It's in my car. I'll get it later."

"You can just keep it, go through it if you want."

I did not want, but I don't say so. Instead I stand up. I'd agreed to help, we'd talked a little, it seemed like an okay time to retreat to my room again.

"And your grandparents will get into town the day before the memorial."

I pause, trying to hide a wince as I avoid glancing at the lurking figure.

My dad's parents had moved to Florida after he died, selling the farmhouse where he'd grown up, escaping to warmer weather and attempting to connect with their estranged daughter, my dad's sister. We didn't see much of them anymore, though I knew my mom talked to my grandma regularly. There'd always been a coldness there, in the farmhouse, in the relationship between them and my dad, in the way my grandpa watched my dad and how they avoided talking about anything deeper than the weather and work, at least when we were around. They hadn't said much at the funeral, and I was a little surprised they were coming for this. I'd always gotten the impression they'd rather pretend they didn't have a son who squandered all the talent he was given, spent half his life in rehab facilities, and drank away any chance at a proper life.

"Okay." I don't really know what else to say. I turn to leave.

"Cal."

I stop and glance back at her.

"It's good to have you home."

I smile. We aren't an "I love you family." We don't hug on every hello or goodbye. But we let each other know we care in small ways, and we'd been through too much with each other to doubt it.

Back in my room, I close the door behind me, fall back against it, bring my fingers to my temples, and sigh.

"You don't look so great, Cal."

I jump. "Please don't do that," I hiss.

"Talk to you?"

Well, preferably, yes. "Sneak up on me."

"Can't really help that." He has one hand in a pocket as he lifts the other and pulls it through his hair.

He backs farther into the room and I move away from the door, needing to keep moving, to keep my hands busy.

Am I turning into my mother?

I can't relax, can't do any of the things I would normally do on vacation, like sit and disappear into a book, knowing I'm not really alone.

Sure, it was my dad but . . . was it? I still wasn't sure how this all worked. And, truth be told, I wouldn't be able to relax even if I knew, without a doubt, this was my actual dad standing in front of me. He wasn't always the most calming presence. Okay, he never hit us or anything, but I'd always known, from probably five years old, that something was off. I may not have known *what,* but when my cousin declared loudly over the phone when I was barely five, "You know your dad's drunk again, right?" I knew it wasn't good. I knew, somehow, that it meant he couldn't be trusted to take care of us, even if he wanted to. I knew it meant he would always be just a little different from all the other dads. I dreaded the rare times when my mom would go out and leave us under his care, even during a sober stint . . . because you never knew when those would be over.

It didn't matter that he was also the one who would play his guitar and sing to me when I couldn't sleep. The nights he would perch on the edge of my bed and sing my favorite songs until my eyes drooped and I didn't notice when he went back to his TV show seemed canceled out somehow by the yelling and the crying and the years of knowing that my dad could not be trusted to take care of me. Maybe that wasn't fair, but that's how it was.

I think about this while I make my bed, arranging my pillows and stuffed animals neatly. Most of the time my bed stayed unmade, much to my mom's annoyance, but I needed to keep moving.

"You doing okay?" His voice makes me jump, again.

I ignore him.

He tries again. "How are things going?"

My hesitancy to communicate with a ghost loses out over the instinctual answer that tumbled out of my mouth every time someone asked this question over the last year. "I'm *fine*."

"The girl in that field didn't look fine."

I flinch. Seems like a low blow to call out a time I was emotional, vulnerable, and on the ground in the mud.

"I had a bad dream. I was upset. That's all." I start pulling clothes out of my bag. "I'm *fine*."

"I don't know, Cal."

I wince at the nickname, the familiarity he seems to slip into so easily.

"I don't think I'd be here if you were."

I spin around. "You're not supposed to be here."

I'm trying to poke a nerve (do ghosts have nerves?), make myself as surly and unfriendly as possible, but as far as I can tell he doesn't feel anything about my statement. He just gives a small nod from his post next to my desk.

"That is true."

"So?" I prod.

"So . . . ?"

"Why are you here?"

He just shrugs and I roll my eyes and go back to what I was doing.

I keep unpacking and he stays silent. But not for long.

"So a memorial, huh?"

I grunt.

"And you're speaking."

"I guess. Not really my choice."

"Well, like your mom said, you're good with words."

"I write stories. Fiction."

"Maybe it's time to write something true."

As I pull clothes out of my bag, the paper with the red ink flutters to the floor. He glances down and sees the statement at the top before I can grab it.

"Looks like I'm not the only one that thinks so."

I toss a glare over my shoulder. He no longer has the right to give me homework advice. Not like he ever did. "The truth isn't pretty. No one wants that."

"What is the truth, Cal?"

I whip around. Was he trying to *shrink* me? "The truth is, you were gone and now you're not. The truth is, *I don't want you here.*"

That one gets him and he looks down at his feet.

I keep pushing. "So how do I get rid of you?"

"Maybe that's up to you."

It was a bullshit answer. Up to *me*? Him being here wasn't up to me. His spending years and years in the bottom of a bottle when he could have been being a dad wasn't up to me. Why would any of *this* have anything to do with me?

"You're the one that decided to go all Casper the friendly ghost. You showed up in that field. *Why*? Why are you here?" I'm sure he knows more than he's letting on.

He sighs. "You asked me to be here, Cal."

"I didn't—"

"On the hill. You called out to me and said you had so much to say. You wanted to tell me something."

"I was being dramatic! I didn't expect the ghost of my dead dad to appear in front of me and follow me home!"

"You asked—"

"Well, now I'm asking you to leave. I am *begging* you."

Maybe I *had* asked him to be here. But all I'd wanted was a sign he was listening. A cracking branch, a gust of wind. *This* was not what I'd wanted, not even a little.

He opens his mouth to answer, maybe to argue, maybe to accept my offer and leave me alone, but before he has the chance, I unmake my freshly made bed and crawl back under the covers. I don't want to deal with any of this right now.

"Please," I mumble into my pillow, "just leave me alone."

Silence fills the room. If he isn't gone, he's at least honored my request. I let out a long breath and let my head sink into the pillow, trying to ignore the throbbing in my temples. I focus on my breathing instead of the prickliness on the back of my neck that indicates I still have an audience. My heart rate slows, my breaths come deep and long, and soon, sleep takes me.

Chapter Four

Didn't mean to destroy the love I wanted to give to you.

E.S.

When I open my eyes, the light in the room has changed.

It's not the soft glow of dinnertime—it's the harsh, bright blaze of early morning. I'd slept through the night. All the way through the night.

I shoot straight up and search the room, bracing myself. But he's not here.

"It was a dream," I whisper, but even as I say the words I don't quite believe them. I don't see him, but something feels different. There's an energy I don't recognize. It's familiar but . . . not.

I shake my head. I'd convinced myself I was going crazy, so now I'm acting like it. I slip out of bed, still fully clothed from the day before. I tilt my nose toward my shoulder and sniff—I really need to change my clothes.

In the hallway, I pause. I was going to head downstairs and do a scan of the house, confirm whether I'd slept my way out of my very own installment of *The Twilight Zone*, but a half a day's worth of sleep has made me groggy, and sleeping in my clothes has made me stinky. I need a shower.

The hot water soothes my aching muscles, and the release of tension clears the cobwebs made of memories and dreams sticking in my brain and slowing my thoughts. I don't think about what might be waiting for me downstairs, but by the time the water runs cold (which doesn't take long in an old house like this), I am certain of one thing—I know without a doubt that whether this is real, a mental breakdown, or a haunting,

I don't want him here. I haven't come to the realization others might in this situation or in the movies—that this an opportunity I need to seize, a once-in-a-lifetime chance to mend fences or close doors or heal. I don't want to seize it.

I also don't want to speak at the memorial, but unless I want one of my mom's famous "I'm so disappointed" looks (and I definitely do not), I can't weasel my way out of that one. And if I can't get out of it, I certainly can't do it with the dead dad I am speaking about watching over my shoulder. That leaves only one solution. So I turn off the tap, dry off quickly, and replace the jeans and sweatshirt of yesterday with another pair of jeans and a long-sleeved shirt with my school logo. I don't dry my hair or bother with makeup.

I step out of the bathroom, and immediately any shred of hope that my real-life nightmare has faded disintegrates. From the top of the stairs, I hear it. A low hum in a familiar tone, crooning a nonsensical tune. I sigh and stomp my way down the stairs. By the time I get to the bottom, I'm expecting it, I really am, but as I come around the corner of the last few steps of the staircase and he comes into view, I jerk to a stop. The scene in front of me is so familiar it startles me.

He's there, waiting for me on the couch. Taking a load off from haunting me all night, maybe. And while I know this morning is different, it's too much like countless mornings before.

Coming around this corner was always a gamble. With the couch and the TV right there, we never knew what we were going to find. Too many mornings I'd rounded these very same steps to find him on this very same couch, sometimes passed out from the night before or already on his way to a good buzz. The TV would be blaring and I would stop, unsure if I wanted to move past him and risk waking him up or attracting his attention.

On the mornings he was awake, I knew what would happen.

He'd hear me coming down the stairs and he'd jump like a startled rabbit, shoving the brown bottle he'd been sipping back under the couch cushions, as if we didn't know it was there. And then, he'd want to talk to me.

Maybe share obscure facts about the film he was watching and slur his way through tidbits about the actors, or even try to have a heart-to-heart, his eyes shining with inebriated emotion. I shake my head as I remember one particular morning, an interaction I still think about, one that haunts me like the man now watching me from the sofa.

That day, like many before, I wasn't in the mood to be the girl with the drunk dad, and I wasn't in the mood for *him*. I just wanted cereal. I wanted to call my friends and get out of the house, but I knew the price I would have to pay to get those things.

I tried to move quickly and quietly, but that morning he wobbled to his feet. "Have you seen this?"

I stopped and sighed out a no, wishing I was a normal teenager irritated by a dad giving me a hard time about how late I'd slept or where I'd been the night before. I wished I was rolling my eyes because I didn't want to talk about it, not because his speech was slurred at nine a.m. on a Saturday.

Maybe it was the fact that he wasn't heading out to tinker in the garage or play ball with my brother or watch sports like other dads, but for some reason, that morning, I was done with it all.

"It's really great." He slurred as though he were talking around a big ball of cotton.

I didn't respond. His words were harmless, but I kept one foot behind me even as I studied him. I cringed as I took in all the details I wanted to ig-nore: His unsteadiness as though he were standing in the middle of a teacup ride. The glassiness of his eyes as he tried but failed to make eye contact. The wrinkled clothes that smelled like yesterday's mistakes.

A waltz danced from the TV speakers.

"The music is great too." He half stepped, half stumbled forward, placing a hand on the arm of the loveseat to steady himself.

I had to suppress a groan as I realized he was trying, and failing, to dance.

I took a step backward, but he didn't seem to notice.

He closed his eyes and started to hum along to the song as the couple on the screen waltzed their way down a darkened street, and I wondered if he'd forgotten I was there.

Before I could sneak away, his eyes snapped open like he just had a brilliant idea.

"Dance with me?" he asked with outstretched arms.

I froze, an almost automatic "no" pausing on my tongue.

I looked from him to the TV, and suddenly two scenarios played through my head as clearly as the movie dancing across the screen.

I *could* dance with him.

I could take two minutes to show my dad that even though he'd put me and our family through hell, he was still my dad, and somewhere deep down, buried under boulders of resentment, I loved him.

I could seize the opportunity, because frankly, it might be the last chance I got to dance with my father. The days of daddy–daughter dances and "not noticing" his weird walk because I was still young enough to pretend I didn't know what drunk meant were over. By that point, he no longer went to family events, so I wouldn't get a chance at a wedding, and honestly, I already knew the odds of him making it to mine.

I should have danced.

I was fourteen, but I could already feel his connection to this life fading as his body rejected the addiction his brain relied on. I knew, without knowing how I knew, that my dad would not be around much longer.

And I was right.

But maybe a dance would have changed things.

Maybe if I'd rested my head on his shoulder, he would have realized I still needed him. I might have been distant and guarded, but as much as I tried to fight, as much as I try to deny it now, a girl needs her dad.

I'd need him to share my love for stories and creativity and really bad disaster movies (because no one else would). I'd need him to tell me what other movies that actor has been in because no one else ever knows. I'd need his kindness, and his certainty that most people are worth spending a little time talking to, because frankly, the world is pretty awful and people are really, really hard to like.

Maybe I could have shown him then and there that his daughter would always love him, even when she hates him...

Maybe that dance could have fixed him.

Maybe it would have given him a reason to fight one more time and made him strong, stronger than the pull of the bottle and stronger than his demons, strong enough to actually win.

Maybe I could have fixed him if I had tried.

Maybe if I'd danced, he would have changed.

But the second I looked away from the TV, the fantasy dissolved and the truth stared me in the face.

I didn't want to smell his sour sweat or rancid breath or hold him up while he leaned against me to keep from falling over.

So, even though I knew what it would do and could already see the backward jolt of his head at my words and knew they might send him back to his bottle, I'd looked him right in the eye and said, "Get sober, and I will."

But he didn't.

And now he's a ghost, standing in the middle of the living room, probably wondering why I'm staring at a blank TV screen fighting back tears, or maybe even remembering the same moment I am, if it wasn't burned from his memory by booze. Part of me hopes it was.

The humming I'd heard at the top of the stairs stops as he stands, cautiously watching me as I stare off into the past.

"Morning, Cal." He's hesitant, unsure if I'm talking to him or I'll ignore him, but one thing is for sure, he's not the man from my memory. He's not holding on to anything for support, his eyes are clear and focused on me, and his words are crisp, his voice steady, deep, soft, and comforting. He's wearing a clean button-up shirt and dark straight jeans and he's almost glowing. No, he's not glowing, but there is a white light surrounding him. A bright circle engulfing him that I'd been too distracted to notice yesterday. I shake my head. This keeps getting worse.

Despite the light, today he's the man he could have been, the man he could have become if he'd set down the bottle, if we'd danced . . .

I shake my head. It wasn't my fault. I know that. But it doesn't make the sting any less bearable. My recognition of my lack of responsibility in the course of my father's life doesn't make it any more fair that the man standing in front of me is the man who could have been my dad, and instead he's a ghost.

I still haven't said anything, and I am still standing in the middle of the room staring at him. My eyes are hot, my face feels warm, and I realize the memory I've been wallowing in has made me emotional.

I clear my throat and look down at the ground. I don't say good morning, I don't greet him like a daughter would her dad, because I don't really know how normal father-daughter relationships should work, but I don't ignore him. I have something I need to say.

With a little less fire than I felt when I'd stepped out of the shower, I manage to squeak out my words around the lump of memories in my throat. "Look, no offense, but I don't want you here." Okay, so maybe a little offense.

His eyes droop, but I ignore his hound-dog expression as he looks up from under hazel eyes. This isn't real or at least it's not my life anymore and I have to be done.

"Cal, you—"

"I know. I called you here. I was tired. I was emotional. I thought I needed some big dramatic movie moment to get closure and stop having wild death dreams, but I don't. I'm good."

No part of me thought that trying to get a few things off my chest would result in my actual dad standing in front of me trying to walk me through a deep life lesson. That is not what I wanted or needed.

"So, how do I get rid of you?"

His smile completely disappears when I complete my question. He hesitates.

But I push. "Look, my mom wants me to speak at the memorial and I can't do that with you hovering. So whatever I have to do to end"—I motion between the two of us—"this, we need to do it now."

"Okay."

"Okay?" I didn't think he'd give in that easily. He was the one haunting me, after all.

"You're hurting, Cal. That's not what I want. I couldn't give you much when I was alive. I wanted to, but I couldn't. I can give you this now."

"You mean you can . . . go?"

"No. Not right now. I've tried."

"You've tried? To leave?"

While I was sleeping? I don't like that I'm annoyed by the idea of him just disappearing with as little warning as when he'd shown up.

"Yes. It was clear you didn't want me here. But I couldn't. Something is keeping me here rather than where I'm supposed to be. But I can help you figure out what it is and when it's time, I assume I'll go."

"Help *me?*"

"Well, it seems like you have some . . . stuff to figure out, and if you do, I might, I don't know . . . poof?" He splays his fingers open and shrugs.

That wasn't the answer I wanted to hear. What was this? Some Hallmark movie with an M. Night Shyamalan twist? *To free herself from the presence of her dead father, Callie must face a past she's always been afraid of.* Oh, that was actually kind of good.

I shake my head. Good for a movie but not my life.

"So, you think I have to go on some journey of self-exploration with my ghost dad sidekick and figure out what emotional baggage is tying you here?"

He laughs, though I don't find the situation funny. "I guess so."

"Great." I think back to all the ghost movies I've watched or stories I've read. "So, we probably need to . . . do some stuff?"

He lifts his eyebrows.

"You know, like a journey or . . . a mission."

"To accomplish what?"

"How am I supposed to know? What are some things you regret from your life—maybe that will help?"

"Cal, this isn't about—"

"You?" I shake my head. "See, that's where I think you're wrong. *You're* the ghost. Ghosts only come back when they have unfinished business or need to accomplish something they didn't do when they were alive. So what do we *need* to accomplish?"

It's his turn to shake his head, and I can tell he's not satisfied with my answer, but he humors me. "Well, I regret all the time I missed with you guys.

There were so many things I wanted to do as a dad."

My skin turns hot and my face flushes. "You *could* have—" I take a deep breath. This isn't about the choices he made or my anger at those choices. "Okay. So we do some of those things."

"You didn't hear anything I said, did you?"

"I heard you, I just think you're wrong."

He shakes his head. "So stubborn."

I roll my eyes and head toward the table where my keys and bag are sitting. He stands and follows me. "This is what we're doing. It makes sense. We'll spend a day doing the daddy–daughter things we never got to do, you'll feel all warm and fuzzy and then move on before the memorial. You can at least try, right?"

His silence says he doesn't agree.

"*Right?*" I press.

"I'll try, Cal."

I accept his acceptance but ignore the tone.

Well, perfect. We're having our first daddy-daughter fight right now. Check that off the list.

"Okay then." I grab my keys.

"Now?" he asks.

I shrug. "The sooner the better. I have to go pick up music at Manny's anyway. We can knock out everything in one trip."

"Sounds good. So what's your plan?" he asks, even though I know he doesn't agree with my strategy.

I haven't had much time to think about it. "I don't know. I guess we have some fun?"

He laughs. "I like fun."

I roll my eyes and that makes him laugh again. Is this how dads and daughters interact?

My mom and brother are already at school. Part of me envies Taylor even though he's sitting in class right now. He might be suffering through lectures on a book he definitely didn't read, but at least he's ghost-free. Maybe I should go get him, drag him along on this haunted journey, see if he has any insight. Why isn't my dad haunting him? I make a note to investigate this when I can stomach the idea of having a brainstorming session with a ghost.

But I decide to let him be. He's a sixteen-year-old boy. What insight into the human, or nonhuman, condition could he offer?

With no one to say goodbye to, I leave a note on the front table, our preferred form of communication when we're all under one roof, saying where I've gone, and head out the side door to the driveway.

It's early enough that it's still chilly, the spring sun not strong enough to offer any relief from the previous evening's chill. I'd left my jacket inside, opting to rely on my long-sleeved shirt for warmth, so I hurry to my car and settle into the driver's seat. Even though I'm not sure I have to, I leave the front seat clear. As I am turning over the engine of the small Honda and pulling my seat belt on, I hear, "Nice car," from beside me.

I gasp and bring my hand to my chest. I'm not sure I'll ever get used to this.

"Why," I whisper under my breath, "can't you use the door?"

"Oops, sorry." He cringes. "But I can't really grab onto anything, so doors aren't an option."

"Right," I say. "Obviously."

I check my rearview mirror, even though our street is as quiet as it always is, before I pull out of the driveway, shaking my head. Every time he says something that confirms his "condition," I am forced to face the reality of our situation, but no matter how many times I acknowledge it, it doesn't seem real.

"So I have to stop at Chuck's and Manny's. You know how to get there?"

"I do. They're both in Lawson."

Awesome. Supernatural navigation. Well, at least it was better than struggling with Mapquest directions. "Okay, perfect. We can do that last."

"So what's first?"

I have a few ideas tumbling around in my head now that I've solidified a plan. Knowing that I could be rid of him in the next twenty-four hours, I'm almost looking forward to trying some daddy-daughter activities with this man in front of me, this Dad 2.0 I never got to experience. But first . . .

"First, I need coffee."

"You drink coffee now, huh?"

"I do work at a café, I have a refined palette." I'd also been drinking coffee every single day since I'd started that job, and even with over twelve hours' sleep under my belt, I knew I'd get a headache if I didn't get some caffeine in my system soon. But I don't tell the ghost of my alcohol-addicted father that. "Well, it's mostly milk and sugar, but I haven't exactly been sleeping well this last year." I give him a pointed look.

"Ah." He nods. "Right."

I glare for a moment, thinking he might take a little more responsibility for the fraught emotional state of his daughter, but he doesn't say anything else, and I realize he may not even know about the dreams. He's a ghost, I guess I can admit that now, but I don't think he's omniscient—at least, I hope he's not.

There is a new coffee shop just on the edge of town where I could get my milk, double-syrup, double-whip, double-sugar latte before heading out toward Lawson, one of the closest cities to our small town. Thank goodness, because only months before, my only option would have been a diner or McDonald's.

My car rolls toward the center of town and one of only two "busy" intersections. There's no light, just a stop sign for me, a gas station on one corner, and the town hall square on the other. If I turned left, I would head into the center of town, a dentist's office, an insurance company, a diner, a hair salon, a four-way stop with a new blinking red light, and a few other businesses that had come in since I'd left and would probably be gone in a few years. And if you ventured a little farther, past the pizza place I was definitely going to have to visit before I went back to school because their breadsticks were to die for (maybe a poor choice of words while sitting next to a ghost), my old high school.

But I was turning right, toward the two main (two-lane) highways that led out of town and into actual civilization, towns with malls and movie theaters and roller-skating rinks and real grocery stores.

To be fair, we did have grocery stores, two at one point, but they were small, high-priced, and not where you went to do your big grocery trips—just to grab a few things to tide you over until you could make a trip into the next town to stock up. Or, if you were my dad, you used them to supply your habit.

For a few years, we'd had a store down the block from us, within walking distance, and before it closed, the owner branching off into other businesses, my dad had been a frequent customer.

The other, just on the outside of town, was still hanging on, and once it became the only option, my dad became a regular there. Frequently stopping by to replace his empty bottles, he would often leave my brother and me in the car, wondering why we couldn't join him and grab some candy or gum, while he "just ran in." It was back when that was still okay, leaving kids in the car (no danger of kidnapping in our small town), but I'd still always felt uneasy about it. Passing it now, I get that same gnawing feeling in my gut as I picture him checking out with a small bottle of Canadian whiskey and a pack of Marlboros, the clerk knowing full well who he was and why he was buying booze at ten a.m. on a Saturday.

I don't know now if he'd tried to buy anything to draw attention away from the bottle, but looking back, I suddenly realize that we were *that* family. We were the ones people whispered about after he'd cleared the double doors. The ones everyone knew about. My face burns.

I don't say anything as we pass, but I glance at my passenger. He doesn't seem bothered. He's looking out the window, studying each new detail, every new addition, and he's humming again. It's another mindless tune, at least to my untrained ears, and I'm not even sure he knows he's doing it. He's happy. Heck, the crooked smile he's sporting indicates he's downright cheerful.

"Knock that off," I say, though I'm not sure why I can't let him have a pleasant drive. One of us should.

He's startled out of his reverie. "What?"

I just shake my head as we approach the curve that will take us first to the coffee shop and then out of town. I pull into the parking lot. Without a word, I get out, leaving him in the car for a change, and step inside the small café.

It's busy for what it is. There are a few people in line and a few taking up the limited seating. I know them all, one way or another, vaguely at least. Even the folks working behind the counter,

I smile at no one in particular, rushing to the line and checking the time on my phone to give the impression I am in a hurry . . . and I am. I'm in a hurry to get in and out before anyone engages me in conversation, asking about school, my mom, and then eventually—

"Callie!" A voice from behind the counter pulls my attention from the fake text message I am reading with interest.

I lift my gaze to the voice of the man who has just materialized from the back room behind the counter. The owner, I presume. It takes me a minute to place him, but when I do, my heart sinks. So this was what he'd tried once his grocery store, the one down the street from me and the one my dad had frequented for years, had gone under—a coffee shop.

"Oh, hey," I say because I cannot remember his name. My mom would know, but she knows everyone.

"It's good to see you. Back from school for a visit?"

"Yeah," I nod. *Obviously.* "Looking for a little pick-me-up this morning."

Is it just my imagination or does his lip give a small twitch before he smiles wider and motions to the menu? "Of course. You've come to the right place. Just let Matt here know what you want and put away your wallet. Your money's no good here."

"Oh no." I shake my head, "That's not—"

"No arguments. After what you all have been through . . . well, I insist."

My face burns again as he nods solemnly. I don't need this man's sympathy or his charity, but I just give a slim smile, pressing my lips together and glancing anywhere but at his face.

Matt looks at me expectantly, not saying anything but also clearly recognizing me either because of my brother or my mom, because his eyes do not meet mine as I give him my sugary, foamy, whip creamy order.

"How's everything—" the owner starts, but I can't do it. I can't take any questions about my family: how are we doing and how are we all adjusting and wasn't it all just so sad and such a terrible waste. I know all of that.

"I'm sorry, but I've got kind of a long drive. Can I use your restroom before I hit the road?"

"Of course, of course." He says it softly, as though I am asking if I can have a moment to sob in his back room, and motions to the door at the back of the café.

I pull the door to the cramped bathroom shut behind me and press my hands on either side of the sink, letting out a deep breath. There's no sobbing, no tears, but my heart pounds and my cheeks burn and thank goodness my ghost dad has taken this opportunity to stay behind in the car instead of following me like a lost puppy.

I splash some cold water on my face and take a few deep breaths. This is why I never come home. This town knows too much about the past I am trying to forget.

I hear a voice yell my order and I know I can't stay in here forever. Maybe if I pretend to be on a call, they'll let me rush back through the café, grab my drink, and head out the door like a busy businessperson who doesn't have time for small-town chitchat because she has deadlines and meetings and more important things to do. But before I can get out my phone and think of a few lines to say, I hear a voice coming through the vent in the ceiling of the bathroom.

"Such a shame," the owner says, and I roll my eyes. Always the same word, the same phrases. People need new material.

"He was the one you had so much trouble with, right?" A woman's voice now. The owner's wife probably.

"That's the one. Bounced a few checks and even caught him stealing once. Told him to get some help and I wouldn't press charges, and he did, I think. Guess it didn't stick, though. That poor—"

I've had enough. Pressing my phone to my ear, I pull open the bathroom door and step into the café, nodding vigorously at my imaginary conversation. I grab my drink off the counter and throw the cash I'd been planning to use as a tip on the counter.

I don't say thank you, and I don't make eye contact with anyone. I just leave.

Chapter Five

But the battle was just beginning, a long way from the end.

E.S.

I slide into the driver's side of my car, slamming the door behind me and setting my drink in the cupholder. He's still in the passenger seat, back straight, hands folded in his lap.

I don't say anything as I throw the car in reverse and press the gas, accidentally (mostly) squealing my tires as I pull out of the parking lot and get back on the road. I can feel him looking at me, studying my red cheeks, my hands gripping the steering wheel and my chest rising and falling as I try to steady my breath.

"How's the dessert coffee?" he says softly, an attempt to reengage me.

"I'm not thirsty anymore."

"Everything—"

"Do NOT ask me if everything is okay. You know full well it's NOT okay. Don't ask me how I'm doing or if I'm hanging in there or how I've been. You *know* the answer to all those questions is '*not good*' and you know that all of it is your fault."

Silence.

The car rolls soundlessly out of town.

"So . . . you're *not* fine?"

I reach over and flip on the radio, trying to drown out his questions and all the things we're not saying. It's on a station that claims to play everything but really just covers light rock, pop, some occasional country, and a lot of Queen.

It's a song I like, a song that came out when I was about eleven or twelve and I liked listening to because it made me feel older, like I was cool and kept up with new music. It was also a love song and

I was convinced I'd be in love very soon so I'd better prepare.

As the female singer bops about the subject of the song always being her baby even after they broke up and grew apart, I notice the ghost's leg tapping along and his fingers drumming the top of his thigh.

I try to ignore him.

I keep both hands on the wheel, trying to fight back the hot tears that burn my eyes every time I let my anger and frustration bubble to the surface. I don't want him to see me shed one more tear over him.

But now that the music is on, he doesn't seem to notice or care that I'm upset.

"The chorus of this song is really interesting. She's really vocally talented. I can see why you like it, she does a great job of—"

I reach over and flip off the radio.

He looks over at me. "What happened in there, Cal?"

"You *stole?*" I want to make it very clear this is not about me.

"I . . . ," he sighs. Whatever he was expecting me to say, that wasn't it. He probably wasn't expecting me to know, but honestly how could I not? This information should not have been surprising to me. He barely worked. If he had a job, it never lasted long—only as long as his latest sober stint, or sometimes longer, depending on how well he could hide his drinking. We got by on my mom's teacher salary, which could have been enough but was definitely not enough to support a family of four *and* his habit. He drank the cheap stuff, sure, but it wasn't free.

"From our local grocery store. You stole from people we knew. People that knew us, that we saw almost every single day."

"I did a lot of things I'm not proud of, Cal."

"And that makes it okay? Because you're not proud of it?"

"No. It doesn't."

Silence falls again. What was I supposed to do with this information?

"It wasn't me, you know that, right? The things I did. It was the alcohol."

"And who drank the alcohol? Who decided, even after months of being sober, to go to the store and even if you didn't have any money, get a bottle, open it, and take a drink, knowing exactly what would happen?"

"It's not that simple."

I scoff. "So I've heard."

I reach over and flip the radio back on. I don't want to hear anymore.

"Cal, I think we . . ."

"What? Need to talk? What is talking gonna do?"

"Please turn it off." He's trying to sound stern, to "father" me.

"No. You had every opportunity to talk when you were here. You had so many opportunities to make things right." Though, even as I say it, I know I'm not being entirely honest. He'd had opportunities to talk to me, yes. And sometimes he'd even tried to take them. Maybe even when he was sober. But my anger and hurt overshadowed any desire I had to unpack his excuses with him, and I never wanted to hear it. Just like I don't want to hear it now.

We drive without speaking for a few minutes, but after gnawing on my bottom lip and considering what the next few days might look like knowing what I know now, I voice a nagging question. "How am I supposed to speak at the memorial?"

"What do you mean?" he asks tentatively, as though he already knows the answer.

"Memorials are meant to remember the good times you had with someone. And right now I'm having a hard time thinking of any."

I'm sure my words are hurting him, but what did he expect?

Even now, driving down a two-lane highway, going just over fifty-five with him in the passenger seat, I'm assaulted by another memory, a day that started off good and was supposed to be about creating a positive memory, kind of like this one, but he ended up ruining by drinking.

We were heading to a hotel we liked to visit sometimes on the weekends. It was a fun way to get away without taking a whole trip. It was far enough from home that it felt like a break but close enough to enjoy for a night without wasting all your time in the car. My brother and I liked it because some of the rooms had balconies with stairs that went straight down into the pool area, and frankly, we thought that was the coolest.

Maybe he'd seemed sober before we left but about halfway to our destination it was clear that my mom had made a smart move when she chose to drive. The transformation was beginning. First, his voice would start to crack, and then slur. He would start to ramble about things none of us really cared about and then badger us with questions we would answer hastily. And then his temper would flare.

My brother and I weren't paying attention at first. I was reading and he was probably playing one of those handheld games that were almost impossible to beat. The radio was on and it seemed like it might be a fun family weekend.

And then, "You shouldn't have even come." My mom's voice, the one that belonged to her when the man she was married to changed, carried into the back. Her transformation had begun too.

My mom was mad, but so was my dad. He wasn't raging, crying drunk yet, just easily annoyed, make-very-bad-decisions drunk.

"Quit it," he said, and tried to go on talking about the song and the artist on the radio. He began quizzing her, tossing out question after question. He nagged and persisted, egging her on when she said she didn't know.

"You're drunk," she finally spit.

"I'm fine," he said. It was the dance they always danced, the game they played that no one won.

"You always have to ruin a perfectly good thing."

"Stop it."

"You're just going to go to the bar when we get there."

"I knew you didn't want me here. You never do."

"That's not—"

"Fine, if you don't want me here, I don't have to be here. Stop the car."

"Don't be ridiculous."

"No. I don't want to be here if you don't want me here. Stop the car, or I'll just get out."

My brother and I glanced at each other, now fully tuned-in, and a silent question passed between us. *"He wouldn't. Would he?"*

He reached for the passenger side door before my mom could react. In just a few seconds there was air whooshing into the moving vehicle and he was holding the open door with one hand and fumbling with his seatbelt with the other.

My brother and I were screaming.

My mom was yelling and trying to keep the car in control and trying to reach over him to close the door. "Knock it off, you're scaring the kids!"

"Don't, Daddy!"

"Stop it, Daddy! Stop!"

I don't remember the rest. I don't remember if we turned around to take him home or if he came with us and did in fact retreat to the bar while my mom, my brother, and I tried to enjoy pizza by the pool. I just remember screaming from the back seat, convinced my dad would soon be splattered all over the highway.

I shake my head. Now he's in the passenger side of *my* car and he's stone-cold sober, though I wonder if he's wishing for a drink as his only daughter makes it very clear she can't find anything good to say about him to a group of his loved ones.

"You have to say what's on your heart, Cal."

"No one wants that."

He scoffs. "I don't know about that. I'm sure half your audience would agree that there's not a whole lot of good to say about me."

I don't respond.

"Maybe *that's* what will get rid of me. You speaking your truth."

Again, I don't say anything. I have a different plan. I steer the car, not into downtown, but onto a back road, a road I'm sure he knows well.

"Callie," he whispers. "Are you . . ."

He can tell where I'm going, so he doesn't finish his question.

I'm done with this little adventure that I never asked for, this second-chance journey I did not need, and I'm ready for some answers.

"It's where you showed up, maybe it's where you need to be to go back."

"I don't think that's—"

"I'm willing to try anything right now." I slam on the brakes at the bottom of the driveway and turn to glare at him. "You said you would try."

He's staring up at the house and he doesn't look at me when he answers. "I will."

At first, I think he's just studying his childhood home, taking in the details as I did when I'd first pulled up to the house . . . was it only yesterday? But then I see he's staring at a sign. A sign hanging from the post where a saw blade used to hang advertising my grandpa's tool repair business. It's still a sign advertising a business, though I can't believe I didn't notice it earlier.

"You've got to be kidding me," I whisper as I read "Harley Cameron, Psychic Medium. Tarot Readings. Healing. Mediumship Readings."

"Well," my dad said, with a small smirk, "that explains a lot."

I roll my eyes. "What does it explain? That anyone can own a business these days? You *believe* in this stuff?"

"Callie. You're talking to a ghost. Maybe she can't see the future, but if she has a connection to energy outside of herself, it could be why I was able to connect with you here."

When I don't respond, my dad nods his head toward the front of the house. I follow his gesture and see the woman who must be Harley standing on the porch and waving, gesturing for us to pull up.

"She sensed we were here," he says, wiggling his eyebrows at me. He's grinning. I don't like how much he's enjoying this.

"Or she heard our car." I offer another eye roll as I push the gas to urge the car up the small hill of a driveway. "Real or not, she knew something was going on yesterday, I could tell. I'm talking to her."

I climb out of the car. I don't wait until I am at the porch to speak.

"You owe me an explanation."

"Hi, Callie." Her eyes twinkle. "It's so good to see you again so soon. I had a feeling you'd be back."

"Of course you did." I don't know if I believe in psychics, but I hadn't believed in ghosts before yesterday, so clearly my go-to state of disbelief isn't going to get me very far in this conversation. But I can still slide in a little sarcasm.

"I'm Harley." She smiles and holds out her hand. I pause. Would she be able to read my mind or something if she touched me?

My dad whispers from behind me. "Callie, don't be rude."

I grasp her fingers and then quickly let go.

Her smile doesn't falter. "Come in?" she asks, gesturing to the door behind her.

I hesitate. "I . . . I guess?"

No part of me wants to go into that house, and even though I'm no medium, I can sense the same hesitancy from the figure behind me.

She begins turning toward the door, then stops. "No. This is not a happy place for either of you."

"Either of us?"

She smiles at me. "Isn't that why you came back?" She motions to the wicker patio furniture strewn about the porch. "We can stay out here. It's a beautiful day."

It is. It's turned into one of those rare spring days in Michigan where the state decides to play along with the season. The sun is out and a cool breeze lifts the hair off the back of my neck.

"Have a seat and I'll get us some tea."

Despite the warmth of the day, I shiver and pull the sleeves of my shirt down over my hands before climbing the four steps up onto the porch.

I don't look behind me to see if he follows. I don't ask if she can see him or sense him or if she knows where he is at the moment or what he's thinking. I'm not sure I want to know the answer to any of those questions, and I'm still not sure I'll believe anything she has to say. She disappears into the house, and I sink into a thick cushion perched on a wide chair.

He is still standing in the drive staring up at the house. Is he remembering the time he'd been staying here after my mom kicked him out and, after stumbling in drunk, was bitten by the family guard dog?

Or was he farther back? Were there happy memories here too?

I don't remember specifics of our visits here, just feelings. Dread. Curiosity. Cold. The smell of a woodstove. The sandpaper feel of my grandpa's beard when he would kiss my cheek. It wasn't like visiting my mom's mom. There was warmth in her home. It was welcoming and accepting. Here, I always felt like a visitor, trying to get comfortable on old furniture, to avoid the dog, to tread quietly around my grandpa or be heard over the blaring TV. I was constantly trying to see into dark corners, to unravel the mystery of my dad, and his dad, and why we all were the way we were. Could this woman offer answers? Did I want them?

There's a softness here now though, I notice as I study the details added by the new owner. Pillows of all colors are strewn across the white furniture, stacks of books lie on a table in the middle of the chairs and loveseat, and patterned tapestries hang between the beams of the porch. Crystals and bells and plants and flowers cover every inch of every surface, and it reminds me of a coffee shop on campus where I like to study and read. My grandpa would hate absolutely everything about it, which makes me kind of love it.

The front screen opens as Harley backs through with a tray, balancing a teapot, two cups, and cream and sugar. No tea for her other guest, I guess.

She sets the tray on the small table and settles into a chair on the other side so we are facing each other. Is she going to want to grab my hands? I stretch my sleeves farther over my fingers. But her hands stay busy as she pours tea into each cup.

"Cream? Sugar?"

I nod. I take my tea the same way I take my coffee.

She hands me a cup and I wrap both hands around it, warming the tips of my fingers. This whole situation is not playing out the way I imagined when I pulled up to the house. I didn't come here to have teatime and sing "" with a psychic (though my dad might enjoy that) and I'm glad she doesn't have a guitar handy. I came here for answers.

She settles back in her chair, sipping from her own cup. Her blond hair is piled on top of her head and the skin around her eye crinkles as she smiles. "So."

"So you knew what was happening the other day when I left, didn't you?"

"I felt a change in the energy around you, yes."

I raise my eyebrows. "Why didn't you say any-thing?"

"I did."

I think back to her cryptic fortune cookie-style statement. "Why didn't you say anything more . . . concrete?"

"Would you have listened?"

I open my mouth to reply and then close it again. I ask another question. "Well, what exactly *is* happening?"

"Isn't it obvious?"

I don't say anything. I want her to say it.

"You have a spirit connected to you. Your father, yes?"

"You can see him?"

"No, but I can . . . *feel* him. Spirits who have already passed give off a very distinct energy. Almost like a ripple in the air. They're not supposed to be here, so they upset the natural balance of things."

"Where are they supposed to be?" I ask.

Harley lifts her gaze to the sky and gestures up with her eyebrows.

"Right," I say. I'm not up for a discussion about the afterlife this morning. "How did you know it was my father?"

"Your feelings are very strong."

I lift my eyebrows and, without thinking, inch away from her.

She laughs. "I can't read your mind or see your thoughts. No need to grab a tinfoil hat. But I am sensitive to the emotions of others, and I do have a strong connection to spirits . . . or they have a strong connection to me. I haven't really figured that out yet." She gives a thoughtful nod and sips her tea. "Whichever it is, when people, or spirits, are experiencing strong emotions, it's like they're a mirror and those emotions are reflected back at me. I don't feel them per se, but I can almost 'see' them in a reflection. Sometimes the mirror is glass and emotions are clear, and sometimes they are more like those fun house mirrors, and I have a harder time interpreting what they're feeling. If that makes any sense." She lifts her shoulders and smiles like she's just admitted she doesn't always put the shopping cart back in the rack.

"And which am I?"

"Oh, you're clear as glass, Miss Callie."

I'm not sure I like that. And her "explanation" isn't really helping me at all. I take a sip of my tea while I think about her answer and my next question. She seems content to wait and crosses one leg over the other while she leans back in her chair. Her eyes dart between me and where I'm assuming he's standing, somewhere behind me but not on the porch.

"He's not a fan of this house," she says quietly.

"No," I mumble, "I don't think he is. So, you said he's connected to me. Why?"

"Why what?"

"Why is he connected to me?"

"You're his daughter."

Thank you, Captain Obvious. "Yes, I know that. But, why did he connect to me in the first place?"

"You want to know why he's here."

"Yes."

Her eyes narrow. "You'll have to ask him that. You . . . you haven't asked him?"

"I have and he doesn't know either."

"Hmmm." She lifts her cup to her mouth, and when she pulls it away, she purses her lips together.

"I mean"—I think back to an earlier conversation—"I guess he said it was because I asked him to be here . . . but I didn't!"

"So, he came because you called, because you needed him."

"But I didn't! And I don't."

"Mmm." She takes another drink of her tea. "Well, it sounds like you have a lot to work out and not a lot of time."

"What do you mean?"

"I mean," she begins and then stops abruptly, her head turning toward the bottom of the porch stairs. "Oh," she whispers. "Okay then."

"Okay then what? What do you mean 'not a lot of time'?"

"Oh, I just mean . . . the memorial. The memorial is on your mind and I imagine it's a sort of . . . checkpoint for you both. It would be wise to have things sorted by then."

"*Sorted?* That's like four days away! I don't even know what I need to do. *What do I do?*"

"You help him."

"Help . . . *him?* I'm the one being haunted!"

"But he's—" She stops again and nods, almost to herself. "You both need each other, Callie. Once you realize that and accept it, things will be much easier."

I jump out of my seat, teacup still gripped in my right hand. "That's it? That's all you're gonna give me? We *need* each other? I have a *ghost* following me around, a real, live ghost. Yes, I heard it," I add because I see her mouth open, "and all you're gonna give me is some cryptic bull—"

"Callie."

I stop talking at the sound of his voice and turn toward him.

"That's enough."

Is my dead dad scolding me? But when I turn back toward Harley, I realize I've been standing over her, yelling. He's right.

I sigh. "I'm sorry. I shouldn't . . . I just . . ."

"I know, Callie. It's okay." She stands up and before I can stop her, she takes my cup, sets it on the table, and takes both of my hands in hers. She's slightly shorter than me and has to look up to look into my eyes, but her blond hair is so tall it closes the few-inch difference. "All you need to do is listen. And feel. And let it in. You'll know what to do."

"Let what in?" I whisper.

"All of it."

My head hurts with the effort it takes to stop my eyes from rolling all the way up into my head, but I hold eye contact. So much for answers. "Okay. Uh, thanks. I think we're done here."

She lets go of my hands and nods. I turn to start down the porch steps.

"Don't avoid this, Callie," she says from behind me. I glance back and she's wringing her hands, watching the air around me. "We always seem to think we have more time than we do."

That, I understand.

I nod and head to my car, my dad keeping step beside me.

We're quiet on our way to our first stop. I guess since my impromptu "return to the scene of the crime and see if things are magically fixed" plan did not pan out, I still need to go through with my original strategy—quality time with my dead dad. Super. It's not the most appealing way to spend an afternoon, and my brief excitement from this morning is already waning, but if it's what I need to do to free myself of this nightmare, I can go through the motions.

"Where are we going now?" he asks softly.

We're both feeling a little raw. It's barely eleven a.m. and it's already been a morning.

I don't answer, but I turn my blinker on as we approach our destination.

The movie theater where we used to go as kids is empty this early, but it's open and plays family movies during the day, movies for stay-at-home parents who need something to do with their young kids while older siblings are at school. I couldn't resist when I called and heard they were celebrating the ten-year anniversary of one of my favorite movies, *Hook.*

"We're going to a movie."

We watched movies at home a lot, but I can't recall ever going to a theater with him, or at least just him and me. I did go to see *Jurassic Park* in the theater when I was only eight, and I'm not sure my mom would have made that choice even though she was there, but the only thing I remember from that outing is hiding my head between my knees every time the T-Rex destroyed a car or ate someone off a toilet.

"And because no one else can see or hear you, you're free to tell me every obscure fact you know about this movie, or the actors, or the actor's brothers. But nothing that will ruin it—it's one of my favorites."

I hadn't looked at *The Wizard of Oz* the same way since he'd had me watch a documentary about Judy Garland.

He glances up at the sign, sees what's playing, and smiles. "I like this one, too."

I already knew that. I did remember a comment from one of our many viewings about how much he liked Dustin Hoffman's version of Captain James Hook. And I had to admit, I agreed.

I park the car and we head into the theater. I try not to think about how strange I must look—a college-aged kid heading into a kid's movie at eleven in the morning by myself.

"Just one, thanks." I say when the kid behind the counter asks. He looks around as if deciding whether it's okay to let me in before handing me my ticket.

"Thanks," I mumble.

I stop by the concession stand and get myself a box of Milk Duds. A shot of sugar to get me through this weird and awkward scenario seems necessary. In the theater, there's a mom with three little ones already settled into the front row. The kids are running up and down the aisle in front of the seats. I head to the very back.

In my seat, I open my box of candy and, without thinking, offer it to the figure next to me.

"Oh," I say, yanking it back, "yeah. Sorry."

"It's okay," he says with a small smile. "It's not the kind I like anyway."

"Oh yeah, you always liked black licorice and things like Good & Plenty, right?" I shudder and stick my tongue out. "Yuck."

He laughs. "Hey, they're classics."

"Classic doesn't always mean good."

He looks like he's going to argue, when the lights dim and the screen flickers on. His attention immediately shifts. He did always love movies.

After we're urged to visit the concession stand and to be quiet and courteous to the other moviegoers (a message I do not think is received in the front row), the previews start. I already know what movies are coming out this summer, so I glance over at him as he gets caught up on what he's missed in the world of movies, and what he will continue to miss.

"Three!? How many movies can they make about those dinosaurs and that park?" he asks. "Didn't they learn their lesson the first time?"

I laugh, but luckily it's drowned out by the roar of the T-Rex as it gets yet another chance to devour dumb tourists and the scientists who were too busy thinking about whether they could, to consider whether they should.

When the preview for *Ocean's Eleven* comes on, I feel my stomach clench. I think he would really like this one and it would be fun to see it with him. My suspicions are confirmed as he laughs his way through the preview and nods along as the premise is outlined.

"That's a remake, you know? I don't know if they can ever top the original starring some of the Rat Pack, but it looks pretty good. You'll have to let me know how it is."

I must look shocked or skeptical, because he leans closer and adds softly, "You can always talk to me, Cal." He winks. "Even when you can't see me."

I don't know what to say, but the previews end and the movie starts, and with the first twinkle of music, we are both captured. Sometimes I forget that we are both writers, storytellers, lovers of a good tale and a great movie. But as soon as the little girl in the play whispers her lines from *Peter Pan,* we are both transported to a simpler time. We watch as a grown-up Peter Pan struggles to be there for his kids *and* have his very important career. We avoid eye contact as his wife tells him how special this time is, when they're so young, and how he is missing it.

We enjoy the opening scenes, but when Captain Hook steps out onto the deck of the ship, his mustache twitching and his hook dancing, my dad can't help but laugh.

"He really is fantastic in this."

I nod my agreement.

The pirates gather to worship their captain, and my dad can no longer hold back. "Watch the pirates. Did you know there are a few cameos?" He tells me that Glenn Close, a friend of Robin Williams, was visiting the set when she was asked if she wanted to appear as a pirate and enthusiastically agreed.

I laugh because I did know that, but I let him tell his story.

When he's done, I decide it's my turn. "Did you know this whole idea came about because the screenwriter's son asked him at the dinner table one day, 'What if Peter Pan grew up?'"

My dad turns to look at me, and even though he missed my graduation and never made it to many recitals and wouldn't be at my wedding, I don't think he could possibly look any prouder than he does in this moment.

"I didn't know that." He nods his approval. "That's great."

For the rest of the movie, we try to out-fact each other.

"Did you know this was one of Gwenyth Paltrow's first movies?"

"Did you know Dustin Hoffman was the voice of the pilot in the beginning?"

"Did you know the couple kissing at the end is George Lucas and Carrie Fisher?"

When the family is reunited, the mother sobbing so hard she is hyperventilating, and Peter delivers his last line, "To live, to live will be an awfully big adventure," I cry.

I always cry when I watch this movie, so I'm sure it has nothing to do with the situation I find myself in or the man next to me who will never actually get the chance to make up for missed time with his children or recapture his youth and life, but I try to hide the fact that I'm dabbing at my eyes anyway.

When we emerge into the sunlight, he stops before descending the stairs into the parking lot and looks at me. "That was really fun, Cal. Thank you."

My eyes are still stinging from the end-of-the-movie emotions and have barely dried when I feel my throat clogging up again, so I fake a sneeze.

He doesn't make me talk. We stand on the steps of the theater for a minute, blinking into the bright sunlight, taking in the warmth of the afternoon.

The parking lot has started to fill as more people head to the attached mall or a matinee.

"You're still here," I say, stating the obvious and blowing my nose with a tissue I found in my jacket pocket.

"I'm still here."

We slowly start walking toward my car.

"What next?" he asks.

"What kind of unfinished business do you have?"

"Callie, what if—?"

"You went to school here, right?

"Yes, but—"

"We could go there. You could show me around. Oh! We could . . ." I trail off and look at the ground. I'd spoken up without meaning to, but there *is* actually something I'd like to do, though I'm a little embarrassed to admit it.

"What is it?" he asks.

I sigh. It wouldn't pay to be shy now. This might be my only chance.

"I've always wondered . . . well, how the heck do you make those really fancy sandcastles?"

He laughs, but he's not making fun of me. It's almost like a bubble of hidden joy tucked away inside him has popped, and that laugh was the sound it made as the joy escaped. "Get in, take us to a beach, and I'll show you!"

"A beach? It's a little cold, don't you think?"

"It's the perfect day! But if you want, I could hang around for a few months and we could go when it warms up."

"All right, all right. Let's go."

Luckily we live in a state filled with lakes both coastal and inland, natural and man-made, and he knows of a small park on a tiny lake with a little bit of sand just outside town.

I nod my head toward the street in front of me, indicating I don't know where to go. "I need some help."

"I'm here." He winks. "For now."

Chapter Six

The world is a beautiful place, given a choice, wish it would stay that way.

E.S.

"You're way too excited about this," I say as we pull into the parking lot of the lakeside park.

He ignores me. He's leaning forward in the seat and yammering on and on about structure and technique and texture. "The sand at the Great Lakes is really the best, but this will work for to-day."

"That's a lot of information about sand."

But his comments provide me with a flash of a memory: a sunny day, cold water lapping at my feet, plastic shovels and buckets surrounding us as my brother and I frantically dig a hole to stop the water washing toward the castle my dad has spent hours working on. Folks walking by gawk and exclaim, and we squeal as the waves get closer and closer. He must have known his work would eventually be washed away, erased, but he'd built it anyway.

We're the only people at the park, which is a bit of a relief. I don't care that much about what people think of me, but a parent spending a nice day at the playground with their kid might call the police on a woman building sandcastles and talking to herself.

"So," I say, motioning toward the clearly man-made square of sand butting up against the water, "what's the secret?"

My dad making sandcastles on the beach was always quite the spectacle. He could create layered turrets on his towers and turn piles of sand into detailed and sprawling structures with towers and moats and decor that looked like someone had poured melted chocolate on top and then let it dry.

"I told you, the secret is in the sand," he says, motioning toward the water. "Weren't you listening?"

I shrug. "Kind of."

He shakes his head and goes on. "It needs to be wet enough to drip. So you have to grab it from the edge of the water, or fill a bucket with water and sand." We don't have a bucket, so we settle in to where the water meets the sand. I kneel and the knees of my jeans are immediately damp.

In the dry section of sand, we make piles we can use as test towers. Well, I do.

"Now," he says, "scoop a handful of wet sand, and try to get a little water in there with it."

I do.

"Make a fist. Hold your hand over your target, and squeeze the sand out through the bottom of your hand."

I do. It plops onto the pile of sand in one big chunk. "Uhhh . . . I don't think this is what we want."

He chuckles. "It just takes practice. Try again. Play with the consistency."

I try a few more times, and eventually my hands remember past lessons, and I manage to get the sand to dribble out through my hand little by little. As it hits the pile beneath it, it creates pebbles that stack on top of each other and start to form little turrets.

"See?" he says, nodding. "It's getting better."

I keep practicing as a gentle breeze tickles my cheeks and the sun warms my back through my shirt. It's so close to being a normal day, a relaxing afternoon shared by a father and daughter, that my heart actually aches a little.

He watches me quietly, providing instructions every now and then, and while he watches my hand, I look up at him and notice something.

"The light," I whisper.

He looks up and around, trying to see what I'm talking about. But I'm looking at him.

"What light?" he asks.

"The one behind you, or surrounding you, I guess? It's . . . different than it was this morning."

I'm not sure how to describe it. Since he'd appeared, I'd been too focused on how to get rid of him to take the time to actually study him, but I had noticed the light this morning and now it caught my eye again.

"Different how?"

"I don't know. Maybe, dimmer? Smaller?"

He shrugs and nods toward the sand. "Oh, who knows."

"Aren't lights pretty important in the whole afterlife situation?"

"The first one, yeah. After that it's all bright white light and harp music."

"It's . . . what, really?"

He winks. "Kidding, Cal. I'm sure it's nothing. Do you want to try a few more? I think you're getting the hang of it."

I look around. The sun is starting to dip toward the horizon. I didn't realize how late it was getting. "We should probably get to Chuck and Manny's."

I stand up and brush off my hands and jeans. I am covered in sand.

"This is never going to come out." I shake my head as I try to get off as much as possible before getting into my car.

My dad nods and follows suit, pretending to brush the sand off his lap. When he sees me glaring, he smirks. "One of the benefits of being dead," he says with a shrug, and I huff at the dark humor.

We head up the beach and toward the parking lot. There's a bench where the sand meets the grass and I didn't notice earlier, but a man is lying across it. He's covered in dirty layers of clothing, and there is a shopping cart next to him filled to the brim with cans, newspapers, and bottles. The bottles in the cart are all empty, but the one on the ground next to him has about two finger-lengths of brown liquid left at the bottom. Whiskey is often described as an amber liquid when it's in a fancy glass with a couple of ice cubes, being sipped by men in suits settling business deals. But when it's the cheap stuff, it can only be described as brown.

I'm about to go around, give him his space, when my dad whispers, "Callie."

I turn around and see he's stopped walking. He's staring down at the man. I backpeddle a little and stop.

"Is he okay?" my dad asks softly.

"Uh, I don't know." He's sleeping on a park bench, so I'm not sure how okay he could be, but I know that's not what he meant.

He looks at me, his eyes pleading. "Can you . . . make sure?"

"*What?*"

"Please, Callie. If he's sick or . . . well, he doesn't deserve to be alone. No one does."

I wasn't sure how he could so confidently make that statement. He didn't know this man. Maybe he was a terrible person. Maybe he was a drunk who tortured his family until they finally kicked him out. Maybe he—

"Cal."

"Okay, okay!" I step toward the man, peering down at his face. His eyes are closed and he is very, very still. "Hello? Uh, sir? Are you okay?"

He doesn't stir and I look back at my dad. He urges me to try again. I step closer and, with one finger, touch the man's shoulder. I try not to think about how dangerous this is and instead focus on the fact that by helping this man it might help my dad move on.

I press my hand to his shoulder and give a firm shake. "Sir!"

He stirs. His eyes twitch and blink open, squinting up at me. With the sun behind me, I imagine he might think he's died and is looking at an angel beckoning him to come into the light.

"Are you okay?"

"Wha—?"

I look back to my dad. He's okay. But he urges me on. "Are you all right?"

"Well, I *was* sleeping,"

Right. I'd be a little annoyed too, frankly.

"Okay, yeah," I say and turn to go.

"Can we call someone for him?" my dad asks.

I sigh. "Is there someone we can call for you?"

He grunts again, squinting at me and then look-ing around. "Who's 'we'?"

"Oh. I mean, me. I. Can I call someone? Family or something?"

He scoffs. "Family doesn't want me around."

I glance at the bottles in his cart and the one beside him. I can smell him from here.

"Yeah," I say, and see my dad shaking his head from beside me. "A shelter or something then?"

He sits up and his eyes finally open all the way. He stares at me. "Why do you want to know, kid? Why do you care?"

I *could* say I don't. Because if it wasn't for my dad, I probably would have walked right past him. But how could I explain *that?*

"I . . . I just . . ." I glance at my dad. "No one deserves to be alone."

The man blinks at me, his already watery eyes shining. He jumps like he's been poked, and I get the impression it's been a long time since someone has said anything like that to him. He opens and closes his mouth a few times, running a hand over the gray stubble lining his chin and cheeks. Finally he coughs out a response.

"I . . . I could use some food."

I look down, patting at my pockets like I would find a sandwich or a granola bar. No surprise, they are empty. I have some money in my wallet, but he asked specifically for food and I'd rather give him that, considering what my dad had done every time he'd gotten a little extra money. I could tell the man I don't have anything for him, or give him the few dollars I have shoved in my pocket, but I was the one who woke him up from a pretty deep sleep, so I felt like I kind of owed him. And then there's my dad. He is staring down at the man, a pained look in his eyes, like it wasn't just a stranger he was seeing on that park bench. I look around trying to decide what to do. We don't have all afternoon to stand here, hovering over a homeless man. Then I see the light of a gas station just down the street.

"Wait here," I say to the man, also shooting a pointed look in my dad's direction. He nods, and rather than follow me as I start to jog toward the station, he sits down next to the man.

I reach the gas station in a few minutes, a little more winded than I would have admitted to anyone, and push through the doors. As I scan the aisles, I ponder why my dad was so drawn to this man. I remember my mom and close friends commenting on the fact that my dad never met a stranger and that he would often pick up hitchhikers or chat with anyone he met, but there wasn't a whole lot he could do for this particular stranger in his current condition. Despite that, I have the distinct impression that he wouldn't have let me pass him by no matter how hard I'd tried. Did he see some sort of alternative future in the man's situation? Had he come close to ending up on the streets at one point or another? Why hadn't he?

But the answer pops into my head immediately—my mom.

No matter how mad at him she was, no matter how frustrated, she never would have let him end up like that man. Not everyone had that.

A few minutes later, I approach the bench again, my arms laden with two sandwiches, a few granola bars, a bag of jerky, and a water bottle.

From my vantage point, I can see the back of the bench and the outline of the two figures sitting in it. The man's gaze is aimed out toward the water, his head bobbing up and down like he's listening to something. Music, maybe? But that would mean . . .

As I move closer, I hear it. The voice I'd avoided for the last year, the voice I once knew so well. My dad is singing. Well, not really. He's humming. His voice is rising and falling, flowing like water from one tune to the next, a gentle vibration that to the casual passerby (someone who wasn't being haunted) might have sounded like the wind.

It should have been impossible for the man to hear him, but as I step quietly around the bench, I see that his eyes are closed and his head is moving with the cadence of my dad's notes and rhythm.

I step in front of them, and my dad stops humming and the man opens his eyes.

"Oh. You came back. Wasn't sure you would."

"Uh, yeah. Are you okay?"

"Oh, I'm fine. I feel strangely good, actually." He looks around him like he's worried someone might be listening, and then he leans a little closer toward me, motioning for me to lean down, like he has a secret.

I turn my ear toward him and lean just slightly closer.

"I know you weren't here, and I know this sounds crazy. But for the first time in a long time, I didn't feel quite so alone."

I glance at my dad, who is smiling. "Not as crazy as you might think," I say and drop my arm full of food onto the bench next to him.

His eyes widen as he looks from the pile to me and back again. "Is this . . . for me?"

I nod. "You said you needed food. I know it's not a lot, I didn't have a lot of—"

"It's more than I've had at one time in . . . I don't know how long." He looks back up at me, his dark eyes brimming with tears. "Thank you. For everything."

I shrug. "Sure. No big deal. I wish I could do more, but I have to . . ." I glance toward the parking lot.

"You've done plenty," he whispers, his voice clogged with emotion.

I start to move toward my car as the man opens one of the sandwiches. I stop. "Are you here a lot? In this park?"

"Sometimes," he says around a bite. "When it's quiet. Don't like being here when there are too many people."

I nod. I can relate to that. "Okay, well. Have a . . . Enjoy." I turn back to my car and close the distance between the bench and the parking lot.

Once we're both back inside the car, neither of us says anything for a moment.

"Okay, well. I guess we should get to Chuck and Manny's," I say, not really sure how to process the past few minutes.

"Right," he says, and then looks over at me. "Thank you, Callie."

I watch him as I nod my acknowledgment, keeping an eye out for any signs this has provided him the closure he might need to move on. But he's still solid and glowing, though not as brightly as before. The sun shines into my car, and if he was an actual figure, it would have bounced off his shiny black hair and picked out the few strands of gray peppered throughout the thick mop. Even at fifty-two, he'd only just begun to go gray. He'd put his body through hell, but his hair had refused to give up its movie-star quality. I find myself wondering when it would have happened. His dad had a full head of white hair in his eighties, so it's not like he was immune. My mom's dad on the other hand was almost fully gray by the time he was forty. Which genes would I get, I wonder, running my hands through my short brown hair.

He sees me watching and seems to know what I'm waiting for—well, what I was watching for until I got distracted by his hair—and he closes his lips together in a flat-lined smile. *Still here.*

"Okay," he says, "let's go."

Chapter Seven

I never meant things to be this way,

but that was way back then.

E.S.

"Callie! Hi!" My dad's friend smiles at me from his doorway and backs up to let me through, motioning me in. "Get in here!"

Once I'm inside he sweeps me up into his thick arms and squeezes, lifting me off the ground a little. I laugh despite my mood. Manny has wide shoulders but isn't that much taller than me. His round face is friendly and always ready with a smile.

"Hi, Manny."

He sets me back down. "Let me look at you." He steps back and shakes his head, his chin-length white hair shaking with more bounce than mine ever will. "As beautiful as your mother."

I look down at the ground, never knowing how to take a compliment except to rebuke it with a self-deprecating insult. "But nowhere near as patient."

"I don't think anyone is. Has she qualified for sainthood yet?"

"She really should." I can't stop smiling. It's good to see the friendly face of the man my dad had played music with for so many years. When I was small, his musician friends, sometimes a band and sometimes just friends he was jamming with, were a frequent fixture in our house. They didn't mind when Taylor or I interrupted and often handed the microphone to one of us or let us give them requests.

My favorite was when they played "Knocking on Heaven's Door." I'd sit on the floor directly in front of them and next to my dad's guitar case and knock on the hard plastic exterior whenever they got to the chorus. It made my dad laugh—and I liked to see my dad laugh. Afterward, I would grab my blanket and pillow and climb into that same guitar case. Before I grew out of it, it was my favorite place to nap.

I realize, with a bit of jolt, that all those memories are from when I was small, maybe even before I started school. I don't remember any of his music friends coming over after a certain point and wonder what changed. But I don't wonder for long. The answer is, of course, there in the back of my mind—he was too drunk, too sick, to play music anymore. I shake it away.

"Chuck's here too." Manny's voice breaks into my memories. "Chuck, get out here, man! When your mom called and said you'd be by today, we figured it would be easier for you to make one stop."

"That's great, thanks."

"We were expecting you a little earlier, though." He looks me up and down, eyeing the sand stuck to my knees and the soaked hem of my jeans.

"Yeah, I . . . made a few stops along the way."

"Callie!"

Chuck and I exchange a hug. He's thinner and easier to get my arms around than Manny but much taller, and we all agree I look more like my mom than my dad and that was probably a good thing and they laugh as they me the rest of the way through the house, into Manny's music room. I look behind me. My dad is trailing behind us down the hall, the pull of old friends and music too strong to resist.

"Forget something?" asks Manny when he sees me looking.

"Oh, no." I turn my attention forward.

"We packed up his guitars already." Manny motions toward the door where two cases are resting. "You want us to get 'em back out so you can look at them?"

I shake my head. It was my favorite sleeping case. "No, that's okay."

"We thought your brother might want to have them."

"Yeah, he will. Thanks." I'd let Taylor take them out and look at them.

"We also have some music your mom mentioned you guys might want. It's just a lot of random recordings, singles, 45s. I'm not really sure what they are, but there's a lot."

"Sounds great." I'm only half listening as I watch my dad explore the perimeter of the room, lost in the familiar controls and setup, running his hand above the instruments stacked along the wall, ready to be played. And he probably could have played any of them at a moment's notice. The piano and the guitar were his specialties, but he could pick a tune on just about any instrument you put in front of him.

"Callie?"

Chuck has been talking and I snap my head back toward him.

"Sorry, what?"

"You want to hear something? Some stuff of his?"

"Oh, uhh . . ." I think about his voice coming over the sound system in the room, the flashback to the days I would sit and listen and wait while he recorded or jammed, sometimes his own music and sometimes covers just for fun.

"Here's one your mom would like to sing to me, Cal." He'd laugh before launching into "Hit the Road Jack," and I'd laughed too but actually agreed with both of them.

I think about the humming coming from the park bench and the tightening it had caused in my chest.

I'm not ready to revisit those days, but I don't want to disappoint his friends.

"It's okay," says Manny before I have the chance to say no. "It was hard for me to hear his voice at the funeral. I get it."

They'd played one of his more popular songs, a single he'd released on a 45, from when his talent and voice were both still vibrant, when the world was filled with opportunity and possibility, when he was still the man everyone fell in love with.

Chuck is nodding at Manny's words, his hands resting on top of a box that was sealed and labeled with his name: *Eddie Shepard.*

But Manny is staring off into the distance. He could have been daydreaming, revisiting a past memory with his old friend, and it could be a co-incidence, but he is staring at the corner where my dad is waiting and watching. I narrow my eyes and study Manny's. They are unfocused, like he's not seeing anything, but the corner of his mouth lifts up into a little smile, a dimple showing in his left cheek. He nods as though some suspicion has just been confirmed.

"Do your best to forgive him, Callie. He didn't mean for anything to turn out the way it did."

I heard that a lot and I was getting a little sick of it.

"Then why did it?" I whisper into the heavy si-lence. It's a vague question, but both Manny and Chuck seem to understand.

"Why does it matter?" Chuck asks softly, and I shrug. It matters to me.

"He was a very conflicted person," Manny says, still staring directly into the corner where my dad's standing. Was he talking to him? Trying to get him to see that he understood?

"He was so talented," added Chuck, "and . . . *feeling* and insightful. Wrote probably one of the most moving Christmas songs I've ever heard. We used to play it during the season, and it would bring the room to a standstill. But when his manager died . . ."

"His manager?"

Chuck nods. "Ed really cared about him and appreciated that he cared back. They were close. He didn't have a great relationship with his dad, ya know?"

I didn't know, not much, but I nod so he'll keep talking. Maybe I'm about to get the answers I need.

"He liked that connection. I think he really needed that father-son-like relationship, and it hurt him a lot when he lost it. So when his manager died, he came in off the road and tried to settle down, have a family, but his inner demons seemed to have another plan."

"Inner demons?" I ask. Surely there was more to this than just a lost friend?

But Chuck shrugs. "Like I said, he was complicated. I think more was going on there than any of us will ever know. All I know was, the guy was an amazing talent and I was lucky to have been able to play with him. But in the end, his demons won and we lost."

Manny pulls his gaze from the corner, where he's been staring while Chuck talks, and looks at me. "You can appreciate that, can't you? That he was fighting something bigger than himself?"

I don't really know what to say.

"Appreciate it, Callie, but don't let it consume you. His demons were his own, and unfortunately his choices impacted a lot of people, including you. But don't let his fight become yours. He wouldn't want that."

I nod again, and both Chuck and Manny seem satisfied by my response, even though I am not completely satisfied with theirs. Everyone seemed content with their own explanations; he was conflicted, he lost friends, he was too feeling . . . but none of it explained throwing away an entire life. If I couldn't get answers from two of his best friends, I was screwed.

Manny reaches out and gives my shoulder a quick before turning back to Chuck. "You got that stuff?"

Chuck nods and pats the box he's been guarding. "It's all right here."

"Great, we'll help you get it all out to your car."

Chuck grabs the box, Manny grabs the guitars, and they both head out of the room, leaving just me and my ghost.

I look over to the corner and raise my eyebrows. "Demons, huh?"

"I never wanted to put any of that on you."

"Well, you did." I leave the room, following Chuck and Manny to my car.

I hadn't locked it, so they were already maneu-vering cases and boxes to make them fit into the small four-door.

"What's this box back here, Callie? Can we put it in the trunk?"

I step up to the car and peek into the back seat, not remembering leaving anything behind when I'd unloaded my stuff for the week. But there on the floor of the back seat, where Manny was try-ing to slide one of the guitars, is an old bankers box stacked to the brim with yellow notebooks and loose papers and folders—the box I'd picked up from the farm. I'd had bigger problems to deal with after that visit and hadn't given the box a second thought. And I didn't have much more brainpower to spare for it now.

"Yeah," I say, "the trunk is fine."

Manny lifts it, and as he does, a few loose sheets of yellow lined paper blow off the top of the stack and onto the ground.

Chuck reaches down and grabs them. "Here," he says, handing them to me. He looks down at the paper as he does and blanches. "That looks like Ed's writing."

"Yeah, it was some of his stuff." I reach out and take the paper, tossing it onto the dashboard of the car. "I'll look through it all later." Maybe.

"Oh hey," I say as I move toward the driver's side of the car, "one more thing."

They stop and look at me, waiting.

"This is kind of weird but . . . do you know that beach park about fifteen minutes"—I look at my dad and he mouths the word *"east"*—"east of here?"

"Yeah, sure," says Manny.

I give them a brief description of the man and our encounter, leaving out a few details. "I stopped by there earlier just to . . . enjoy some time by the water and ended up talking to him and getting him a little food. Would you mind"—I tuck my hair behind my ears, fidgeting—"getting him some food now and then? Ya know, if you're over there and happen to see him? Maybe talk to him a bit? He seemed kind of . . . lonely."

To my surprise, neither of them looks surprised by my request. Chuck nods and Manny smiles and points his index finger at me. "You're more like your old man than you think you are."

"We'd be happy to, Callie. Not a problem," Chuck adds.

I ignore the insinuation that I'm like my dad and open the car door. "Thank you, guys, for helping with this stuff, and for the . . . extra help."

"Sure thing, Callie. And you'll remember what I said, right?" Chuck asks, slamming the back door to my Accord.

I nod. "Sure thing."

Back in the car, I fiddle with the radio, trying to decide which piece of the day to address first or if I even want to address any of it. From homeless people to inner demons, it has already been quite a day, and I'm still no closer to getting rid of this shadow than I was at the start of it. Before I can decide if I want to talk, my shadow speaks up beside me.

"I hope you heard what Chuck said."

"That you had demons? Yeah . . ."

So, he'd had demons. Everyone did, really. Mine had jet-black hair and rode with me in the passenger seat of my car.

"No, about not letting my fight become yours. Don't let what happened with me, *to* me, consume you."

"A little easier said than done, wouldn't you say? Ya know, with you sitting right next to me, having this conversation when you're supposed to be dead? Talk about demons. A good ol' fashioned haunting can really mess a girl up."

I was riffing, doing what I always did when conversations got hard and trying to make the situation funny, or at least less serious. He lifts his eyebrows. He's not having it.

"And how am I supposed to prevent it when I don't understand it? If I don't know *why* it all happened?"

"That's why you need to figure out what's going on, why I'm here. I love being here with you, getting to see how your life is going and your mom and your brother . . . but like you said, I'm not supposed to be here. I made my choices. Now you have to make yours."

"But *why*?" I snap, gripping the steering wheel. "Why did you make those choices?"

He's quiet.

"Chuck said something about your dad. What was that about? Grandpa's not the friendliest but—"

He laughs at that. "No, he's not the friendliest, that's true."

"And that made you drink?"

"There's more to it than that. He . . . I wasn't what they wanted in a son. I was never what my dad thought a son should be." He smiles a little and shakes his head, looking down at his lap or back to his childhood maybe. "I started getting interested in art in elementary school. I liked drawing better than hunting or fishing, and that pissed him off. But nothing topped the time they got called into the principal's office and had to come have a chat because I'd been drawing naked ladies during class."

He looks up at me and smiles. "They weren't called in to praise my newfound talent, that's for sure."

He chuckles and I smile a little. I can see him as a scrawny little kid with his thick mop of black hair and his sharp features smiling to himself as his hand glided across the paper, transforming lines on a page into a shape, into a person, into a woman. He might have even laughed to himself a little, surprised at his own creation, and turned to the boy next to him to show off, proud of his work.

It was a cute story. But it didn't explain anything.

"So you were an artist, not a hunter. And Grandpa didn't like that?"

"Grandpa didn't like much about me. Things were different back then, Callie. They were changing, sure, but my dad, he still lived in a world where men were . . . men. They were laborers and strong and stoic. They weren't artistic. They didn't write songs about their feelings—heck, they barely acknowledged they had feelings. They didn't get on stages to sing or dance for an audience. They used their hands to provide for their families, not create. There were men who did, sure. But men like my dad had names for those kinds of men."

I nod and hold up a hand. He does not need to elaborate. "And Grandpa thought you were one of those men?"

"I think he was afraid I was, yes. I think he was ashamed of me, though he would never outright say it. He never outright said much. But when I performed, did plays at school or in the community, neither of my parents ever came."

"Not even Grandma?"

"Grandma did what Grandpa said."

So he had an insensitive, overbearing father who thought he was too . . . feminine? It was sad, and I was sorry his talent was never embraced by his family, but from what I'd heard and knew about the generations before me, this was fairly common. Most parents of boomers thought anyone who went against the grain was a rebel. They thought men embracing art and beauty was frivolous. There was no room for that in their world. It was sad, yes. But it didn't send them all to the bottom of a bottle.

"I'm sorry," I say, and I am. Despite our history, both of my parents had always accepted my desire to write. When I was little, my dad even helped me write a story about the bunny that lived under our shed in the backyard. He helped me craft a tale about a strange sound in the night that scared a little girl and later turned out to be just the family cat trying to get in from outside. In a different world, the man sitting next to me could have been the perfect parent for me. He could have done all the things his dad never did for him. Nurtured our talents. Supported us. Let us know he was proud of us. Instead, somewhere along the way, he'd turned to a bottle for the support he never got from his dad and, in turn, ended up depriving us of the father he could have been.

So while I couldn't relate to some of his story, there was a part I connected with. "I'm sorry your dad wasn't there for you. I know how that feels."

Silence.

"I need to get gas." I turn the car sharply, before we pass the only gas station until we get back into town. As I do, the paper I'd tossed onto the dashboard on the passenger side slides across the smooth surface, coming to a stop in front of me.

"Subtle," I say as I unbuckle.

He shakes his head. "I didn't do anything."

Not sure I believe him, I nevertheless grab the paper before getting out of the car and slamming the door behind me.

I lift the gas nozzle, and after paying and placing it in my car, I look down at the paper in my hands. It's yellow, wrinkled, and faded. The writing is familiar, not only because it was my dad's but because I'd inherited his chicken-scratch style. I was continually grateful that most of my schoolwork could now be done on computers.

The first sentence tells me exactly what it is.

Ed was a nice man with a kind heart who will be missed by some but not by all of the people that knew him.

It's an obituary . . . that he'd written about himself. It must have been an exercise, written during one of his many rehab stints. I look up to where he's waiting in the car, but he isn't looking at me, he's looking straight ahead, his gaze soft, his eyes fixed on the trees blowing in the breeze across the street.

Those of us who knew him well understand how he suffered and how other people suffered for him. He did many good and kind things for many people but could never seem to help himself.

Perhaps he just couldn't believe anyone really cared about him or saw all the good he kept hidden inside. And so to find some sort of peace from the rejection and pain he felt, he turned to and lived for the quick relief that only alcohol could give. When alcohol would treat him unkindly, he would give it up for a while, almost becoming the person he so wanted to become.

The gas nozzle clicks off. The tank is full, but I can't stop reading.

Unfortunately, the real world was too hard or his love for alcohol too great to give it up. He died in the

embrace of that seductive, clever, and patient lover,
never knowing or caring about the good times
with family and friends that could have been.

Hot tears sting my eyes and my chest tightens. My lower lip trembles and I bite down on it. There's something about seeing those words in his writing, the truth spelled out right in front of me, to him from him—he knew what he was giving up every time he took a drink. He knew what he was risking and he didn't care. He knew what it was doing to him and to all of us and he did it anyway.

We who loved him pray he has found the peace
he sought but could never find.

There are dates scribbled at the bottom, the dates that would be his life if he didn't get control of his habit. I choke back a sob. He had himself dying one year before he'd actually passed. He knew what it was doing to him. He knew he would leave behind two confused teenagers and a frustrated wife. He knew it would kill him.

He knew.

A horn blares, pulling me from my ruminations. I'm taking up one of only two pumps at this rural gas station, and it's clear my gas is done pumping. I look up, taking a deep breath to calm my heart, to stem the tears that are threatening. Gripping the already fragile paper in one hand, I grab the gas nozzle in the other and shove it back into its pump.

I move to the driver's side, slide into the car, and pull out of the gas station.

I see movement out of the corner of my eye and can tell he sees the paper crumbled in my hand, my red cheeks, my trembling lower lip that I just can't seem to get under control. He chooses to stay quiet.

We drive in silence. I know the way home so he doesn't need to guide me, and I'm still processing what I just read, trying to make sense of it all; trying to match the easygoing, laid-back man next to me who seems to care so much about his daughter's well-being with the man who was so wrapped up in his own insecurities that he'd rather face death than face the realities of his life.

We pull into town, but at the four corners I don't turn toward my house. I'm not ready to go home. I'm not ready to talk to my mom about seeing Chuck and Manny or to give my brother the music which he will immediately want to dive into. I am not ready to face the family that my dad knew he was pushing away every time he took a drink.

He notices the change in direction and asks, "Where are we going, Cal?"

"I don't know," I whisper. But I sort of do.

Chapter Eight

I'm not in control, I can't even control me. Only God delivers, he seems to be on a break.

E.S.

I don't know that I know where we're going until we get there and I pull over. I didn't actually make the decision, my hands just turned the wheel, my heart pounding against my chest. He looks surprised, and honestly, I am too. This is not usually where I come to find comfort, or come at all unless my mom is dragging me on a Sunday morning or for a dinner or social event she's volunteered for.

I walk up the steps of the white building and am surprised, though I'm not sure it's pleasantly, to find the doors unlocked. I'd half hoped they would be locked, and I'd have to turn around and go home to stew in my bedroom like a normal teenager. But maybe churches never close.

The smell hits me first, and I am immediately reminded of itchy clothes, fake smiles, and distracted doodling. It's the smell of old people, incense, and cleaning supplies. It's the smell of boredom and confusion and obligation. I glance at the paintings on the wall, the paintings that haven't changed in twenty years, probably longer, and the glass case my mom helps keep decorated based on the season or holiday. I pass the pictures of white Jesus and the white men and women who helped start and grow the church. As I pass the book that holds the names of members of the church who have passed over the years, I don't bother to stop to look for the familiar name—I know it's there.

I step into the sanctuary, pausing to admire the way the afternoon sunlight streams in through the stained-glass windows and dances across the wooden pews. There are chairs on either side of the wide entrance for the ushers who are too old to stand while they greet everyone and hand out programs.

I make my way down the green carpet of the center aisle. I don't have to look, I know he's following me. It's strange knowing he's behind me, because the last time I was here he was at the front of this very aisle, in a casket.

The casket was closed by that point, thank God, sparing the funeral goers from the sight I'd been subjected to at his visitation. The closed eyes that despite everything I'd ever heard did not make him look like he was sleeping, the waxy yellow skin, the man that was not my father, not any version of him good or bad, lying there in that small room. I'd stepped in for a moment, my mom guiding me, urging me toward my chance to say goodbye before the other guests arrived. But there was no one to say goodbye to because the body in front of me was not my dad. I'd turned and left almost immediately and avoided the room for the next two days.

I go to the front pew, the same pew where I'd sat between my mom and grandma while the minister spoke of his life and his accomplishments, but very little about the reason he was no longer with us. I'd looked down the whole time, not bothering to stop the tears streaming down my face, twiddling my grandma's diamond bracelet. That was the last day I cried, I realize. Not just fought back tears while a few still managed to slip down my cheeks, but a real cry. After that I didn't want to spare another minute for the thing I'd done so often while he was alive.

In fact, immediately after the funeral, on my walk home with a friend who lived down the street, I stopped at my old middle school to have a chat with a teacher. I still think about that poor woman's face when she realized where I was coming from and that I must have looked insane, talking to her like it was any other gorgeous spring day, but there we were. That was just me, processing feelings by ignoring them.

And I'd spent the rest of the summer continuing to ignore those feelings. Throwing myself into finishing my senior year, preparing for graduation and college. Packing this life away and barreling into a new one as quickly as I could.

But these feelings, all these emotions being brought up by his sudden appearance and visits with his friends and his writings, were now refusing to be ignored, and I was exhausted from trying.

I slump down into a pew. He doesn't ask, just sits down next to me. I don't bother trying to calculate why he can't turn knobs or grab handles and can walk through walls but is solid enough to sit on a bench or in my car. My head already hurts.

We sit beside each other in the front pew of the empty sanctuary. I'm glad it was open but also glad no one else is around. I don't know what I hope to accomplish coming here, but I was always taught church was somewhere you could go when you were feeling lost. And even though my relationship with God has always been tenuous at best, especially over the last year, I am definitely feeling lost.

Lost in my feelings, my anger, and my resentment. Lost in the past and scrambling to see some way toward a brighter, more hopeful future.

"Do you remember when you told me you didn't believe in Hell?" he asks, his voice echoing, at least to me, under the high ceilings and bouncing off the stained-glass windows.

I nod. I've probably thought about that conversation at least once a day since we'd had it, and maybe more since he'd died. I don't know what made me say it that day. I'm not sure I realized I felt it until I blurted it out. But there in the middle of the church, waiting for his choir practice to start, I'd decided to declare my disbelief in the bargaining chip that was supposed to keep Christians in line and prevent men like him from behaving the way he'd behaved his entire adult life.

"Do you remember what *you* said?" I ask.

He nods and repeats the words spoken by the man he used to be. "For my sake, I hope you're right."

I'm surprised he remembers, but maybe my statement had caught him off guard as much as his response had startled me. What was a girl, barely a teen, supposed to say when her dad practically told her he was sure he was going to Hell? I hadn't made a sarcastic remark or a snide comment. In fact, I hadn't said anything. Instead, I did something I rarely did in those days—I looked into his eyes. They were sad, probably still glassy from his last drink. It was impossible to tell at that point whether he was completely sober or if he'd had a few. The fact that he didn't look sick, shaky, or nauseous probably meant that he'd already had at least a few pulls from the brown acrid bottle of Canadian whiskey hidden under our couch. He wasn't drunk, he just needed it to function.

In the years that followed, especially after his death, the fact that my dad, the singer, the songwriter, the man who put on clown costumes for our birthdays and sang "They Say It's Your Birthday" for us at all our parties (whether we wanted him to or not), would only escape Hell if it did not exist was never far from my mind.

I guess it was never far from his either.

"It meant a lot to me that you said that."

I shrug. Even if there was a Hell, I still didn't think he'd go there. What would God have against my dad anyway?

If anyone had reason to wish ill will on the man seated next to me, it was the flesh-and-blood people in his life. We were the ones who faced his mistakes every day, who watched him let go of the thin strings of sobriety tying him to a normal life time after time. We were the ones who suffered because of his choices, maybe not in the heat of the fires of Hell, but on the edge of a life of ever-looming uncertainty—we suffered, yet we forgave. Or at least, we tried . . .

I glance over at him. "You didn't need to worry, did you?"

"Well, I wouldn't go that far. But no, everything turned out okay."

I nod, not realizing how much I'd needed that confirmation. I swallow around a lump in my throat. "Good."

"It's strange being back here," he says.

"For me too. I haven't been back since the funeral."

"You never really liked coming, did you?"

I shrug. "It was fine. I don't think I ever really felt what I was supposed to feel, though."

"What do you mean?"

"I don't know—about God, about Jesus, about . . ." I glance quickly over at him and then away. "About forgiveness."

He nods. "I know what you mean. My relationship with all that was always complicated."

"You always seemed like you believed."

"I was a performer, Cal. That's what I did. I needed something bigger than me to believe in, a higher power that would take everything I was going through and make it make sense, so I pretended."

"So you never really believed?"

"Would you say you've *never* believed in God?"

"I wouldn't say never, no."

"Exactly. I always knew there was"—he gives a quick jerk of the chin—"something out there. Something bigger than all of us."

I nod again. I don't ask if he could now confirm whether that was true, or tell me exactly what was on the other side. Suddenly the answer to that question doesn't seem as important as it once was.

I change the subject. "I did like being here sometimes, though."

"When?"

"When you sang."

His eyes slide toward me, but I don't turn to look at him. I think about all the times I watched him on the altar, singing a solo, and how those were the times I was proud of him, the times I was reminded just how talented he truly was.

Without another word he stands, on steady feet, and makes his way to the front of the sanctuary. I watch as he finds the place that would have been his if he'd been here performing with the choir on Sunday morning, and I sit a little taller.

My dad takes a breath, closes his eyes, and re-leases the opening lines to "Amazing Grace." Goose bumps immediately prickle my arms. They played this song at his funeral, and hearing it now, sung in his tenor, is like a shock to my system. My closed-up, guarded, tightly wound, surly system.

This is it. *This* is where I've always found God, where I felt connected to my own higher power. I didn't find Him through the minister's words or in the giant wooden cross hanging above the altar. I didn't feel Him with me back when I stood over my bathroom sink trying to muffle my sobs and praying as hard as I could while my dad screamed at my mom to give him back his bottle. I didn't feel Him even as I talked to Him, pleading with Him over and over to make it stop, to make us normal, to *help* my dad.

Sitting in wooden pews, listening to the minister talk at us about God and His capability to forgive, but also about the very real possibility of an eter-nity of punishment for earthly sins started to feel wrong a long time ago, and I constantly struggled to feel God's presence. I didn't feel Him inside these four walls, and I couldn't understand why my father, who had made monumental mistakes in his life but was still caring, kind, sensitive, gentle, and devoted to his God in many ways, was worried he was at risk of eternal damnation.

But I felt Him when my dad started to sing. When he shared the voice that you knew was a rare gift, whether in a church, on a stage, or from the edge of my bed on a sleepless night, the icy grip my dad had on my heart melted for just a moment. I felt Him because this must be what it was like when God spoke to you—this eruption of goose bumps as his sweet baritone filled the room and the warm feeling of contentment washed over me. For a brief, peace-filled moment, his strong voice quieted the drum of anger that constantly pounded within me and everything was okay.

While I never knew what an average day with him would hold, when his voice was clear as glass, it was impossible to picture his shaky hand barely holding on to a cigarette. When his words were as smooth as the wood of a shiny black guitar, it was hard to imagine that sometimes we could barely understand his slurred speech. When his eyes were shining with pride and passion as he did this thing he'd always loved, it was easy to forget the darkness that came over them when the demons were fighting within him, because in his voice you could almost hear Heaven.

And now he isn't drunk, he isn't gone. He isn't a specter haunting my days or a nightmare haunting my nights. Standing under the cross hanging from the ceiling, surrounded by a soft white light, he *is* the angel he always resembled when he sang. Why he's here now, I don't know. He's just here, and as he sings, I know it doesn't matter if there is a Hell or not, because no matter what my dad had done or what mistakes he'd made, I know there is no way God would reject one of his angels.

And I know I need to be closer. I need to be the kid I once was, sitting cross-legged while he played the guitar for me and my classmates, friends who thought I was so lucky to have such a cool dad. Maybe I'd agreed with them.

I stand up from my seat and approach the steps leading up to the altar, the steps where we used to gather for children's storytime during Sunday service. I fall to my knees on the carpeted steps, and as I hit the ground, something breaks within me. I am wrapped in the warm blanket of his voice, and more aware of his absence over the last year than I've ever been.

My head is suddenly too heavy to hold up, filled with the years we'd had *and* the years we'd lost. Filled with every question that plagued me throughout my life with him and every fear that followed me through my days. My heart is so heavy, laden down with every conflict that arises when I miss him or hate him or want him with me or am glad he is gone. Everything is so, so heavy.

But his voice makes me feel lighter.

"That saved a wretch like me . . ."

His voice and words drift over me, and I drop my face into my hands and let go of everything I've been holding on to over the last year and during our short journey together, releasing the weight of it all. I embrace the unfairness and release my anger. I let sadness press into my chest and grief escape through racking sobs. He doesn't stop to comfort me, but he does kneel next to me. From beside me, he keeps singing about being lost and then found, and grace relieving our fears. I let his voice relieve my fears and his presence attempt to save me.

And then the song is over.

His voice fades and my sobs begin to slow. I don't look up, not yet ready to meet his gaze. Not ready to face my reality.

And then a new voice makes me jump. "Callie, are you okay?"

I wipe my hand across my face and turn to look behind me. Standing in the entrance of the sanctuary is my old friend Anne. Anne who was a devoted churchgoer and who always had a faith I admired even when I didn't understand it.

"I don't mean to interrupt."

"Sorry." I sniffle. "It was just the song . . ."

"What song?"

Oh yeah. Oops. "Uhhh . . ."

"Can I sit with you?"

I nod. "Of course."

I stand and move to a pew so I am not a sobbing heap on the floor, and she settles in next to me, her shoulder pressed to mine.

She doesn't tiptoe around what might be causing my nervous breakdown on the floor of a church and I admire that.

"I miss hearing him sing here," she says.

I let the tears fall freely down my face. There's no point in holding them back or hiding them now. "Me too."

"He really had the voice of an angel. It makes sense he is one now."

I don't look at him, the man who looks nothing like an angel but can still sing like one. "Seems more like a shame he can no longer share that voice with the world," I say, not so easily comforted.

"I know," she says, pushing her shoulder against mine, "but God always has a plan."

I scoff, I can't help it. Some plan, putting us all through this. "I guess He didn't like *my* plan."

"What do you mean?"

"I tried to pray. I prayed a lot, but I don't think He was listening."

"What makes you say that?"

"I prayed as hard as I could for God to end his suffering, to make him better, to *save* him." I sigh.

Anne turns to look at me, placing a hand gently on my shoulder, and I'm surprised by the intensity and gentle resignation in her eyes when she says, "Callie. He did."

I suck in a breath and look up at the altar. He is still there and there's no denying it, he is the man he once was. That song, that was the voice of a man unaffected by years of hard drinking and smoking and demon-fighting. It was the voice that had landed him the title "a Troubadour in a new age," and earned him the right to play music with Elvis's band. The man I'd just heard singing was a free man. Free from whatever demons chased him to the bottle. The man I am looking at now is clean and strong, and unburdened.

And I realize she is right.

We drive back to my house, only a few blocks from the church, in silence.

Anne, who was also in the choir, warned me that practice would be starting soon, and I knew without her saying it that she was giving me time to get out before a group of boomers who had once known my dad converged with their sympathy and worry and well-wishes. We hugged goodbye, and I tried to press all my gratitude through my arms and into her, gratitude for her company and her words and her warning.

When I pull up in front of the house, Taylor is waiting out front. I'd texted him I was on my way and would need help carrying stuff inside. But I'd sent the text before my impromptu visit to the church.

"What happened to you?" he asks as a greeting.

"Good to see you too." I avoid his gaze, hoping he doesn't notice the swelling and redness that probably hasn't faded on the short drive from the church. I don't care if my brother knows I was crying, but I'm not sure I want to explain that it was because our dad's ghost was singing the song they'd played at his funeral in church while I sobbed at his feet. He already thought I was crazy because of how much I read and how little time I spent outside when we were younger—I didn't need to confirm his suspicions. "There are two guitars and a couple boxes."

He heads toward the car and I add hastily, "I'll get the box in the trunk." The box the obituary had come from, the box of his things. Things I was now suspecting might be able to give me the answers I'd been searching for.

I grab the box and a guitar, and he grabs the other guitar and the box full of his music.

"Did you really need my help with this?" he asks as we head up the walk toward the front door.

"Saves me a trip, doesn't it? What were you doing that was so important anyway?"

He just shakes his head.

"That's what I thought."

He's already got the screen door propped open, and he pushes through the front door, the door that hasn't locked since we moved in but we never bothered fixing because it was so warped that it basically molded itself shut if you shoved it hard enough and any burglar would have woken up the whole house before he was able to break in. Not that there were any burglars in our town.

We step into the front room and I suggest leaving the guitars here. My mom might want to display them near the piano he spent so much time on.

"Okay, we can take the music up to the spare room and go through it, use the CD player in there if we need to."

I nod, still holding the other box.

"What's that one?"

We head toward the stairs.

"I'm not sure," I say. "It might be some of his writing? The lady that lives in the farmhouse now gave it to me."

"The farmhouse? You were already there?"

"Ma asked me to stop by and grab it on my way home yesterday." A favor I was now seriously regretting.

Upstairs in the room across the hall from Taylor's, a room that's been a playroom, a bedroom for various cousins that have come to live with us over the years, a hangout/music room, and is now just sort of a catchall room with an extra bed and a CD player, we drop the box on the floor and pull up some carpet.

"Did you volunteer to do this?" I ask as I lean back against the single bed while my brother reaches for the box of music and starts to explore its contents.

"I guess? Ma said it might be nice to play some of his music at the memorial and asked if I'd like to pick something. I didn't really want to tell her no, ya know?"

I nod. I did know.

There is movement over Taylor's shoulder, and a figure blocks the doorway for a moment before moving farther into the room. The movement draws my attention to the doorway, and I can see through the hallway and directly into Taylor's bedroom. Another guitar, one that my dad must have had here, was propped up against Taylor's nightstand.

"Have you been playing?"

"A little here and there. Just teaching myself the basics."

I see my dad smile from where he's settled near the small window along the wall to our right.

"That's cool I guess."

"There's a lot of stuff in here. Even some 45s."

"Well, we can't play those in the field."

"No, but we can listen to them here."

"What about the CDs?" I was too tired to go downstairs to the record player. I may have loved choreographing dances to *Grease* and rocking out to Hank Williams Jr. on the player in our basement just a few years ago, but I didn't have the energy for the move or the memories. "We'll probably need to pick something from one of those, so we should look there first."

"Those aren't really labeled. We might have to listen to see what's there."

I don't think I can handle hearing his voice again today, but there's no way to explain that to my brother without telling him the whole story. Maybe I should, I think. If anyone had a chance at understanding, it was him . . .

"Cal?" Taylor is waving his hand in front of my face. "Are you okay?"

"I'm fine." It's such an immediate answer.

"Well, you don't look fine. I can just do this myself. You don't have to help."

"No, I . . ." I think about telling him. Really consider it. I look to my dad, who is watching us like we're his favorite TV show. He lifts his eyebrows but doesn't seem to know what I'm considering.

In the end, I lose my nerve. "Why'd you start playing music?" I ask instead.

Taylor makes a face like this is the silliest question he's ever heard. He can arch one eyebrow just like me, just like our dad, and he does. "I don't know. I just did."

"For *no* reason?"

"Not *no* reason."

"Because of him, then?"

Taylor shrugs. "A little, I guess. I've been listening to music more. Some of his music. And it's kind of like . . . a connection?"

"Are you mad at him?" I blurt out the question, and I know it catches Taylor off guard, because his head shoots up from the record he's studying, but I have to know. It's eating at me. I can't be the only one feeling like this, can I? Though, I am the only one being haunted, so . . .

"Ummm, I don't know." It's such a boy answer.

"You don't know?"

"I haven't really thought about it, I guess."

He hasn't *thought* about it? I've been haunted by my anger and guilt day and night for the last year. I've lost sleep, cut off contact with my family, retreated into myself, attracted a ghost . . . and he hasn't *thought* about it?

I don't know how to respond. I'm just staring at him, my mouth slightly open, and he shifts uncomfortably.

"Well, what *do* you think about?" I prod. "I mean, about him? Do you . . . think about him?"

This conversation is already awkward, but I am acutely aware of the man eavesdropping from the corner.

Taylor shrugs again. Was this how he and his friends talked to each other?

"I guess I haven't really thought much about him," he says in a rush of breath and his cheeks turn a little pink. He doesn't know we have company, but he seems to feel guilty about his answer anyway.

Well, at least I'm not alone in my guilt. I look toward the corner. My dad's lips are pressed into a straight line, but he's nodding slightly.

"I've just been . . . busy? Sean and I have been skateboarding a lot. We hang out here—we couldn't really do that . . . before. Things are just so much easier. And I don't *have* to think about him, where he is, what he's doing, what he'll be like the next time I see him. So, I don't."

"At all?" I'm jealous.

"Well, a little. When I play music, I guess. But, that's the good stuff. That's what I like to think about."

The good stuff, I think, wishing I could remember more of it. There was his music and his voice, sure, but surrounding those kernels of warm memories, for every good and positive thing I pull from the depths of my mind, there is an equally scary, sad, or fear-laced memory.

There were beach trips, and snow days spent sledding. There were blanket forts. And indoor campouts. Games he let us play when he was feeling more like a real dad.

Like the night my mom was out for the evening, so my dad said Taylor and I could build a pillow fort in Taylor's room and camp out there for the night. Those were the nights we could forget the real world and escape, slip into a world of pretend. Where our fort was a tent and our house was the *great* unknown, not the uncertain unknown we were used to.

But even on nights like that, the real world usually found its way in. And even our forts, even when they felt like fortresses, couldn't protect us from it.

On the night that has weaseled its way to the surface of my memories, our fortress stretched the entire length of Taylor's bedroom and we'd used every sheet and blanket from his bed, my bed, and the linen closet to construct it. It was glorious. And we got to pile pillows on the floor, curl up in sleeping bags, and pretend we were having an adventure all from the comfort of our own home. My dad even came up with his guitar and sang a folk song, just like we were around a campfire out in the woods.

That was pretty awesome.

We drifted off, almost convinced that we could hear crickets, and that if we poked our heads out the door, we'd be surrounded by blankets of stars rather than actual blankets.

We were awoken by the truth.

"Beverly!" came the bellow of a wild animal. But it wasn't an animal. It was the voice I dreaded, the voice that came from deep inside *him* and meant that my real dad was gone. "Where is it?"

Drawers squealed open, floorboards creaked. And then the door to my parents' bedroom opened.

"Be quiet." My mom tried to calm the savage beast.

"Tell me where it is and I'll be quiet."

My mom's voice was low as she hissed, "You're going to wake up the kids."

The beast once again demanded to be fed.

"I didn't touch your bottle. You probably drank it."

"Yes you did, I know you did! Tell me where it is. Tell me!" He punctuated his last statement by pounding his fist against a table. It shook the whole house.

Taylor woke with the shaking, and we stared at each other in the dark, wondering if our fortress could protect us from approaching dangers.

The springs in the couch creaked. The beast rested and then spoke softly, the whine of an injured animal who was sure there was no escape from their torment. "Please . . . ," he begged. "Just tell me where it is." His voice cracked, and broke; there was a strangled gasp. I wasn't sure what was worse—this or the shouting.

Then came a moment of silence. Taylor and I were frozen, waiting for the next sound, the next sign of movement below. We knew it wasn't over, it wasn't time to relax. Not yet.

And then it came. "I'm goin' to the store."

My mom's protests were muffled as she tried to hold on to hope that we were still asleep.

"Gimme the keys."

We heard her clearly then. "No! We'll get more in the morning. You're not driving."

"Where are the keys? Dammit, I will tear this house apart if you don't *give me the keys.*"

There was a pounding on the stairs. The steps were too swift to be his and we both sat up. The door flew open and my mom was silhouetted against the hall light. She leaned down and pulled back the door of our fortress. "Get your coats. Bring a blanket. We're leaving."

After a flurry of sweatshirts and blanket-dragging and pillow-grabbing, we were downstairs and moving toward the front door. He had already pulled the couch cushions off the couch and was digging through the drawers of an end table. I didn't know if he was looking for his bottle or the keys. I wasn't sure he knew. But when he saw us, none of it mattered.

"Where are you going?"

"Away from you."

The wounded animal cried. "No, please. You can't take my kids."

"We'll be back when you've calmed down."

"No!" He shuffled behind us but couldn't stay steady long enough to move as quickly as we did.

My brother clung to my mom's hands and I kept close to their heels as we all reached the door.

"You can't take them. They love me. My kids love me."

My mom jerked the door open, and I whipped around, facing the creature pursuing us.

I took a deep breath. Some animals only back down when faced directly, when you show them you're stronger than they are.

I took aim. "Not like this." I sounded stronger than I felt. "We don't love you when you're like this."

He reared back. The shot hit its intended target.

We stepped out the front door, into the cold dark night.

I sigh out a shuddering breath, trying to escape the memory that has clawed its way from the depths of my brain.

I look up at Taylor. Does he not remember any of that? "You're really not mad?"

"What's being mad gonna do?"

Damn. When did my brother get so zen?

I don't have an answer, so I just go back to pawing through the music.

"Ma said you're going to say something at the memorial?" Taylor asks.

Now my head shoots up. *The memorial.* My speech. I look toward the corner of the room and meet my dad's gaze.

"Let it in. Listen and feel." That's what Psychic Harley had said. To get rid of him, maybe I needed to do the thing I really didn't want to do, the thing I thought I couldn't do.

"Yeah," I say, still looking at my dad, "I guess I am."

He gives a small smile.

"What are you going to say?" Taylor asks.

I sigh as desperate sobs and shouts and pleas echo in my mind. "*That* is a really good question."

Chapter Nine

Through a forest of trees made of human beings, I came following a path that was cut there.

E.S.

I have a new mission.

Operation: make memories with my ghost dad has turned into *Operation: find something nice to say . . . and mean it.* It might take some research, but I know just the place to start. I leave Taylor looking through music after we decide that the song we played at the funeral would be the best to play at the memorial.

I step into the hall, ready to head to gather the box and face what might be in it.

Before I can move down the hall, my mom appears at the bottom of the stairs. "Hey, Cal, you guys wanna get a pizza for dinner? Maybe watch a movie?"

"I . . ." I think about the task awaiting me and the work I'll need to do to get ready for the next phase of my plan, and my mom's suggestion sounds way more appealing.

I lean back and poke my head into the room where I've just left Taylor. "Pizza and a movie?"

He nods and stands up.

Thirty minutes later, all three of us are on the couch, a large salad pizza (a local delicacy) and puffy, doughy breadsticks with a creamy cheese sauce cover the coffee table in front of us.

"Cal, go get us some plates and silverware," my mom says, "we're not animals."

My brother snorts like a pig and I laugh but stand up and head to the kitchen.

When I get back, my dad has joined the party. I'm surprised it took him this long, honestly.

He's watching them interact, laughing when they laugh, shaking his head at the story my brother is telling about the new skateboard ramp he and his friends built in the driveway (the one that eliminates an entire spot and forces us and visitors to park on the street) and the tricks he and his friends want to try.

He's enraptured by their existence. He doesn't turn when I come up beside him, but he knows I'm there because I hear him whisper, "He's growing up so fast." I nod slightly. One year makes a big difference when you're a teenage boy, and my brother has grown a few inches and lost some of his baby fat over the last year. He's growing into the build of my mom's side of the family—big, stocky guys you wouldn't take on in a fight—but his nose is taking on the shape of my dad's, the same one I've inherited, much to my chagrin. His hair is the same sandy blond of my mom's dad (before he went completely gray).

My mom spots me and motions me over to the couch. "Hurry up, Cal."

As I join them again, I realize we haven't sat like this in a long time.

"Anything good on?" I ask, sitting down.

"Haven't looked yet," says Taylor, and reaches forward to swipe the remote off the table, presumably to prevent me from making a grab at it.

With my dad standing in the corner, it almost feels like we should be watching *Full House* or *America's Funniest Home Videos*, some of our favorite family shows.

As he continues to watch wide-eyed from the corner, I am struck by something as well. He's observing a family he hasn't seen in almost a year, unless he can check in every now and then from wherever he's gone, but I too don't really recognize the family in front of me.

We are relaxed, at ease. No one is glancing at the bedroom door, wondering when it might open to reveal a sick man on unsteady legs searching for a cigarette, or worse, a bottle. We're not trying to be quiet to avoid waking him because he's been throwing up for the last few hours and finally fell asleep.

My mom is laughing. Really laughing. She's talking to her children without glancing over her shoulder. Her newfound ease makes her edgy demeanor of the last few years even more obvious. Her shoulders are relaxed, her smile is real and not pinched, and her eyes are dancing, not tired or sad. My dad wasn't the only one who changed when he dove into a bottle.

We know we can stay here all night if we want and there is no chance we'll need to grab the keys to keep them from him or get in the car to flee the house because he's too far gone to reason with. It's a strange sort of freedom, one we have never known as a family.

My brother pauses on a classic movie channel. I glance over at the figure and see his eyes light up.

"He likes this one," I say, and my mom turns to me. "I mean, liked." I haven't reminisced much over the last year, and she smiles and squeezes my arm.

"He did. He loved all these old movies."

"And horror movies," my brother adds.

I roll my eyes. "Yeah, he's the reason they don't scare me. He explained how they make fake blood and how they did all the effects. Took the terror right out of it."

My mom laughs and my dad gives a small smile. "Isn't that a good thing?" she asks.

"I don't know, I kind of like to be scared. But I guess I had bigger things to be scared of."

My dad's smile fades and my mom sighs from beside me. I wince. I didn't mean to ruin the moment.

"Sorry," I say. "It looks like this one is just starting. We can watch it if you want. Seems appropriate."

"It does," says my mom.

So, we watch. We devour the pizza, and Taylor finishes off what my mom and I can't—there are never leftovers with a teenage boy in the house. My dad hums and sings along with the movie, and I try not to roll my eyes at him. We all laugh together, and sometimes it's almost like they know he's there with us, and I wonder if they've always felt that same presence that I'm only now coming to recognize and appreciate.

Somehow, despite all the sleep I got last night, I'm exhausted when the movie ends. My eyes are already drooping when the credits start to roll, and I am jolted awake by Mom's voice chanting, "To bed, to bed you sleepyheads!"—a refrain she'd often used to shoo us upstairs when we weren't cooperating at bedtime. But neither of us argue now as she gives us each a hug and nudges us toward the stairs. The shadow following me up the stairs almost has me convinced I've lost time in my sleepy state. When I plop down into bed, I'm pretty sure I feel the mattress sink down next to me and I hear a low hum bouncing around the room. I fall asleep with a smile on my face.

This sleep is not the deep, dreamless sleep of the night before. I don't know what happens in my dreams, but I jerk awake in the morning convinced I've missed a deadline for school or forgotten something important.

I look around, trying to place my surroundings. I'm not at school so I haven't missed work. It's spring break so I haven't missed an assignment . . . yet.

"Hey, Cal."

I jump, even though I shouldn't.

That's the feeling pushing against my chest. That's the thing I need to do—get my dead dad back where he belongs before he drives me nuts. That and write a story that will convince my professor not to flunk me. And write a memorial speech that will convince my mother I'm *fine*. And I have three days to do it all.

No big deal.

I yawn and swing my legs over the edge of the bed. There's a Post-it stuck to my bedside table.

Running errands and meeting some friends for lunch. I know you're a coffee drinker now so there is a small bag and your dad's old coffee maker on the counter. Could not get Stormy to leave your room. She must have missed you. Love, Mom.

I scoff and look over to see Stormy fast asleep under the desk chair where my dad has chosen to "sit." It's definitely not me she missed.

"Big plans for today?" he asks, but I just grunt. "Oh, right." He nods. "First, coffee."

I tap the side of my nose with my finger and stand. I grab my notebook, the scratched-up paper, and a pen from my backpack on a whim, trying to grasp onto a cautious hope that coffee and the peaceful breakfast nook in our kitchen will inspire some brilliant ideas.

In the kitchen, I find the coffee my mom left. I guess I should be grateful my dad was a coffee drinker and we still had the pot handy, but I'm actually a little uncertain on how to get coffee out of it. At work, I mix up large pots at a time, and they have the measurements laid out for us. I haven't the slightest idea how to break those down into just a few cups—math was never my strong suit.

"Cal." He appears next to me, slowly crackling into existence like one of those old TVs being turned on. It's a testament to how weird this whole thing is that I don't jump or even gasp when he materi-alizes right next to me. "The instructions are on the bag."

"Oh," I say, moving forward, "right."

After a few minutes, the pot is bubbling and the kitchen smells like coffee. I pull down a mug, filling it almost halfway with milk and sugar before adding the coffee and moving to the table.

I grasp the mug in both hands and take a sip. I can't stop the sigh of delight that escapes as the hot liquid coats my throat. I continue to sip while staring at the blank page in front of me. My dad chooses a spot across from me at the table.

He allows silence while I empty my first cup and get up to get another. He's learning quickly.

Finally, my head still down, I lift my eyes to look at him. "You're still here." It's not a question or an accusation.

"Isn't that what you're working on?" He mo-tions to my notebooks.

I shrug. I should be.

"Or are you working on that paper for school?"

I shrug again. I should be doing a lot of things. Instead I'm having coffee and making conversation with my dead dad. Now there's a messed-up story idea. I shake the idea out of my head, not even able to imagine trying to get the experiences of the last few days down on paper.

My dad tilts his head. "What was that?"

"What was what?" I look behind me and around the kitchen.

"You had an idea."

"Not a good one."

"You don't know that. Want to tell me?"

"No." I definitely do not. I stand up and move toward the counter. "I . . . . There's been a lot going on lately. I feel like I don't have any space to think. I just need more coffee and some quiet time." I sit back down. "Can you give me that?"

"Of course, Cal."

But the quiet doesn't help. The red lines and white of the page scream louder in the silence. The phrase "devoid of feeling" pounds in my head like a drum.

Time passes. I hold my pen. I sip my coffee. Nothing happens.

I drop my head to the table and groan.

I expect a chuckle, an inquiry about my well-being which should definitely be in question. Instead I hear . . .

"I'm proud of you, Cal."

I yank my head off the table. "What?"

"I'm proud of you."

"For what?"

"For what you're doing. All of it. School. Your writing—"

"But I'm . . ." I motion toward the paper, the red scribbles, my own blank page.

He shakes his head. "It doesn't matter. You're doing it, Cal. You're following your dream. You're pushing through even though it's hard. And it's *really* hard. I know. So"—he shrugs—"I'm proud—of your writing, your words, your creativity. I always have been. And I just wanted to make sure you knew, because I'm not sure I ever said it when I wasn't . . . well, you know."

I try to tell myself it's silly, that blind pride just because I'm his daughter and doing the bare minimum isn't real, but tears spring to my eyes anyway and I look down at the table.

He's right. I don't think he ever said it when he wasn't drunk, and if he had, I probably assumed he'd been drinking. I want to embrace his words, but instead I see words from the paper I'd read earlier flash across my line of vision: "*He died in the embrace of that seductive, clever, and patient lover, never knowing or caring about the good times with family and friends that could have been.*"

Did he really even care that he'd never told me?

I swallow around a lump in my throat, "But . . . you followed your dream and . . ."

"You're not like me. You're stronger."

I don't feel strong.

As though he can hear my thoughts, he continues, "There are a lot of different types of strength, Callie. You've had to be strong your whole life and it's not fair, but—"

"Wait"—a thought hits me—"you were a writer."

He narrows his eyes. "Yes."

"You've probably been through this." I wave the paper in front of him.

"Of course. All creative people—"

"Well, what did you do when you were stuck?"

He laughs a little, then lifts his eyebrows.

"What? I . . ." And then it hits me. "Oh. Right. Well, I guess that's what Hemmingway did."

"And he shot himself at sixty-one. Probably not the best strategy."

"I guess not. Oh! What else is in that box?" I'm hesitant to dig back in, considering what I'd found earlier, but something tells me I'm going to have to eventually, so I might as well get it over with.

"I don't really know, but . . ."

I stand up. "Well, I guess there's only one way to find out."

The box is upstairs in my room, but before I can head out of the kitchen, the phone rings. I debate letting the machine get it, since it's most likely a telemarketer or for my mom, but at the last second decide to turn around and pick it up.

"Hello?"

"Hey, Cal." It's my mom. I glance around and realize I'd left my own phone upstairs. "You're home."

"Yup, haven't run away yet."

"Great. Listen, my lunch was canceled and I've been running around all day. Any chance you could get an early dinner together for us? Taylor will be home after practice."

Dinner? How long have I been writing? Or, more accurately, staring at nothing—luckily as a writer, they can be the same thing.

"Uhhh." I hesitate.

"Unless you want to take care of some last-minute details for the memorial?"

"Dinner it is."

After I hang up, I glance helplessly around the kitchen, wondering if ramen noodles or mac and cheese would be okay with my family, because that's about all I've been making the last few months. My stomach grumbles and I realize I haven't eaten much of anything today either. My go-to easy meals don't seem very appealing at the moment, here at home, in this house, but I know what does.

"Hey"—I turn around to face where he is still sitting at the table—"wanna help me make dinner?"

He smiles.

After a quick trip to the store, I gather the ingredients he says I'll need to make his "famous" spaghetti sauce.

I laugh when he calls it that and ask, "Who was it famous with?"

"Well, you guys seemed to like it!"

I roll my eyes. It wasn't hard to impress me with spaghetti. It's been my favorite food since before I can remember. But now, thinking about it, maybe it was my favorite because his sauce was so good.

"Okay, the sauce is the hardest part."

"Is there a recipe I can follow?"

"It's my recipe."

"But didn't you write it down?"

"No, I just knew what to add."

"But what about measurements?"

He shakes his head. "I never measured."

"But how am I going to know how much to add?"

"Don't worry, I'll guide you. Once that's almost done, we'll get the noodles going. You know how to cook noodles, right?"

I scoff. "Of course I know how to cook noodles. I just . . . boil the water . . . right?"

He shakes his head. "It's too bad I never got the chance to teach you how to cook."

I don't point out that's exactly what he's doing now.

He instructs me on how to cut the onion, and my eyes water and swell up immediately, and I swear I will never use onion in anything I cook ever again.

"I don't even like it that much anyway," I say, rinsing my eyes in the sink and sniffling.

"You won't taste it. It just brings out the flavor of the other ingredients."

"Well, then I'm definitely not using it again. Let's just use more of the other stuff."

He shakes his head. "You're hopeless. Open the tomatoes."

I do. Then I cut up garlic and, per very specific instructions, the rest of the ingredients.

He continues. "Now my secret is the simmer. And some secret spices to give it a little kick. We should let it simmer between one and a half to two hours, but no longer. Too long and it burns off all the good flavor."

"Two hours?" I exclaim.

"What's two hours?" says my mom coming into the room and stopping in her tracks. "And what have you done to my kitchen?"

"Oh, sorry." It does look as though a tornado has roared through. I've pulled every spice out of the cupboard looking for what I needed; there are garlic and onion skins fluttering across the counter, pushed by a gentle breeze coming in through the open window; and it looks as though I've used every single dish we own.

I step back and survey the damage, wrinkling my nose. I shrug. "Let's make Taylor clean it up. I cooked."

My mom looks as though she's about to counter that argument with the fact that while she generally cooked all the meals, she was almost always the one to clean up as well, and then she spots the sauce.

"Are you making—" Her eyes fall on the giant pot now simmering on the stove. "Daddy's spaghetti sauce?"

"Uh, yeah . . . I was just in the mood for it."

"How do you know how to make it?" Her eyes scan the countertops. "He never wrote it down."

"Oh, he, uh, told me it once, I think? And I guess it just stuck?"

She narrows her eyes. Nothing has ever "just stuck" in my mind that wasn't related to books, writing, movie quotes, or random trivia I had absolutely no need for. Not appointments, not chores she asked me to do, not multiplication tables. She doesn't press the matter, though, apparently too grateful I am doing something related to my dad without being pushed.

"Well, I think he would be very proud. Sounds like we have a little time, though. I'll help you start cleaning and get a salad made while the sauce simmers. Set a timer. He always hated it when it simmered too long because it—"

"Burns off all the good flavor," all three of us say at once.

She smiles at me. "That's right."

I shove all the food littering the counter into the trash as she pulls out ingredients for a salad.

"How's the speech coming?" she asks, knowing full well I do my best work at the last minute but not knowing that I still had absolutely no idea what I was going to say about my dad, except that maybe he made a great spaghetti sauce.

"It's coming," I say vaguely.

"It doesn't have to be a masterpiece, Cal. Or a novel. I just . . ." She sighs. "I just want you to remember that there was more to him than his drinking."

"But that's all I remember," I whisper as I stir the sauce at his silent urging.

"You remember his spaghetti."

I shrug.

He waves a hand at a bottle of some spice still sitting out on the counter and motions toward the pot. He squeezes his finger and thumb almost all the way together to indicate just a smidge, and I sprinkle a little in until he frantically waves again.

She's watching me and laughing. "I bet you remember more than you think. It's almost like you've got his voice in your head telling you what to do."

I force a laugh. "Almost. But not quite."

I move from the pot back to the counter and continue putting things away.

"What would *you* say?" I ask it so quietly there's a chance she didn't hear me, which is kind of what I'm hoping.

She does, though. She hears everything. "In the speech? That's really up to you. I want you to—"

"No. Not in the speech. If you could talk to him right now. Or if you knew he was listening, what would you say to him?"

She stops cutting cucumbers and turns to face me. She doesn't even hesitate before she says, "That I forgive him."

"Just like that? That easily?"

"Oh, Cal. It's not easy."

"So, you're not mad?"

"Of course I'm mad."

It's not the answer I'm expecting. "But . . . *what?*"

"There are so many things to be mad about and I feel those things on a daily basis. But being mad doesn't mean I can't forgive him. And besides, the forgiveness is just as much for me as it is for him. He's at peace now. He's free from everything that caused him pain. I'm the one—*we're* the ones that have to continue to live. He doesn't need our forgiveness, but *we* need to forgive him. So I do. I just hope he knows that, wherever he is."

My mom is really smart and strong and usually right about most things, but as I watch my dad's face as she speaks, I think she's wrong about this. I think he does need our forgiveness, whether he knows it or not. Because the second the words leave her mouth, he sighs, and as he sighs his form shivers, the light behind him gets a little brighter, and he closes his eyes and whispers into the kitchen, "I love you, Bev."

She gasps a little and brings her hand to her chest, tilting her head. "Did you . . . ?"

I step toward her and grab her hand. "He knows," I say, giving a little squeeze. "I think he knows."

She nods and swallows, squeezing back before dropping my hand and turning back to her veggies. "I love you, too."

If I hadn't been standing directly behind her, I wouldn't have heard it. I pretend I don't as I turn to him, wondering if this is what he needed. Will he cross back over now that he knows his forgives him for everything he put her through for so many years?

But after his quick shiver, his form has solidified, the bright light has dimmed, and he feels more present than ever. He's still here and he's not going anywhere.

"What about you, Callie?"

"What about me?" I ask, grabbing a towel to dry the dish I'm holding.

"Do you think you can forgive him?"

"I . . ." I could *say* it and maybe that would be enough. Maybe he would hear the words and finally have the closure he needs to cross back over, finally rest, and leave me alone. I could say it, but would I mean it? "Like you said, it's not easy."

"No, it's not. But remember, you're not doing it for him. You're doing it for you."

I shrug. It doesn't seem that simple with him standing over my shoulder, listening in and watching my every move.

She turns around again when I don't answer. "You know, it's okay to be mad. He'd understand."

I nod, but I'm not sure I believe her. I'd seen his face when I told him I didn't want him here. I heard the hesitation in his voice when he told me I had to say what was on my mind no matter what that was. Despite what she says, it sure doesn't feel good to be this mad. And as much as I thought I wouldn't care, it doesn't feel good to know he feels bad.

The salad is done and the mess from prepping the sauce is gone. I tell my mom to go relax, and when the sauce is almost done, I add the meat to a skillet and cook the noodles, with a little more supernatural help than I'd ever admit to anyone. Well, at least I know how to do it now. My roommate would be impressed.

The timer goes off and he urges me to remove the sauce from the heat.

"It smells amazing," I say, lifting the lid and giving it a final stir as directed.

"That's a good sign," he says, and I realize he can't smell it.

That's a little unfair, I think as I realize he can't really experience much of the world he's visiting. He can't feel the spring breeze or hug any of us or smell fresh-cut grass or his own spaghetti sauce. Well, all the more reason to send him back. While I'm sure he enjoys watching his family, what kind of "life" is that? Always observing from afar, never able to enjoy the smells and sensations of the lives unfolding around him?

The smell of the sauce attracts the rest of my family without needing to call them, and soon we're all grabbing plates and silverware and serving ourselves from the steaming pot of sauce and the bowl of noodles. We get drinks and napkins, and without being prompted or agreeing to it out loud, we sit around the table.

It's been a while since we've been here, and I find myself wishing they knew he was here, part of a family dinner again and completely sober. He's not sick or sweaty or shaking, slurring his words or yelling at—

Taylor gestures dramatically and knocks over my glass of milk in the middle of his story. Its contents surge across the table, spreading quickly, soaking my mom's placemats and the extra napkins we had in the center of the table.

"I'm sorry," he says quickly, but I barely hear him as my head jerks toward the end of the table where my dad has been standing and observing.

His mouth isn't moving, but I swear I hear his voice, almost as though it's echoing from inside of a cave. *"Goddammit, Taylor."*

I flinch and even though the figure in front of me stays stoic and silent, the echo continues. *"Don't you ever stop to think before you do something? Why would you do that? How can you be so stupid? You need to think, do you hear me, **think!**"*

The voice isn't the one I've grown accustomed to over the last few days. It's the one we dreaded, the one we hid from if we could and tried to ignore when we couldn't. It's the one that could make my brother's cheeks redden and his eyes water. *"Don't cry about it,"* the voice insists. *"Don't just sit there. Do something. And think next time."*

"It wasn't me." This time it *is* the soft, gentle voice of the man that's been following me around. He's watching Taylor scramble to sop up the milk and my mom reassure him that it's fine, it was an accident, but it's like he's not really seeing the moment in front of him but hearing the same echoes I am.

"It was my dad coming out." He shakes his head. "It's no excuse, I know that, but . . . I could always hear him, yelling or scolding, or . . . worse. Nothing we ever did was good enough, ya know? And he told us, he told me, all the time. And I took it out on Taylor. I was too hard on him and he didn't deserve it. It wasn't his fault."

"It wasn't *your* fault," I whisper. I'm talking to him, suddenly trying to convince him that the sins of his father weren't his, but Taylor looks up from cleaning.

"What?" he whispers, because there's no way he can know who I am actually talking to.

"Please," my dad croaks from next to me. "Please tell him."

"It wasn't your fault," I say, this time to Taylor. "When he would yell at you. I think . . . I think he'd want you to know that."

Taylor stares at me as though he's never seen me before, but I don't know what else to say or do.

"You do know that, right?" I need to be sure he knows. We both do.

Taylor nods, ever so slightly, and I think I hear him mumble as he dips his head and goes back to cleaning, "I know."

Chapter Ten

I looked and the trees were swaying

in the wind and sometimes they broke

'cause they didn't bend.

E.S.

I'm lying in bed in the dark. Dinner has been put away, dishes cleaned and counters wiped. Taylor helped clean and we jokingly pulled glasses back every time he got close to one. Laughter filled our kitchen this evening, and by the time I came upstairs, intending to look through the box I'd finally stashed in my room and work on my speech, I was exhausted. I knew I didn't have much time, I knew there were things that needed to be done, but even just the idea of reading the thin lines of my dad's scribbly handwriting made my eyes prickle.

"We have plenty of time," I'd said, staring down at the box but longing for my bed, my explorer streak suddenly much thinner than it had been just hours ago. I looked to him and he smiled.

"We have time," he said. "You need rest."

I nodded, ignoring the fact that two days wasn't really that much time, sure I'd fall asleep as soon as my head hit my pillow.

But I didn't. The events of the past few day had drained me, but my head and heart were fighting against everything I'd learned—old emotions and resentments still bubbling at the surface and the new revelations trying to soften their edges. And of course, the reality of spending time with a ghost was still a bit much.

Now the house is quiet. Taylor came upstairs and settled into his room just a few minutes ago, and I'm alone with a ghost in the dark. His presence is already familiar, comfortable, but my brain won't settle.

"Tell me about your dad," I whisper into the dark.

"My dad? There's not much to tell."

I see where I get my avoidance techniques. "You said he did worse than yell or scold."

"Well, don't get me wrong, my father was not a *total* bastard, he just acted that way most of the time."

I snort. The tone of his voice has shifted, and I can tell he's going into performance mode, but I let him continue.

"He was, after all, *a true* outdoorsman."

"An outdoorsman?"

"A hunter. Tough. A provider. A soldier even." He sighs in the dark. "Maybe he should have never come back from Alaska at the beginning of World War II to marry my mother and join the navy. He saw action that maybe changed him. I don't know. He *did* tell me all the stories."

"What kind of stories?"

"Stories that proved what kind of a man he was, what kind of a man he thought I should be. But from the very earliest, he always stopped me from telling *my* stories. And I don't remember him ever saying encouraging or kind things to me. I do remember learning to hunt and shoot and fish, even though the lessons were a bit harsh. I *did* find myself having fun sometimes and becoming quite good, and that did seem to please him. But most of the time nothing my mother, brother, sister, or I did was correct. And then he'd scream and yell and sometimes he would even hit my mother."

"He hit Grandma?" I whisper. She was so small, so thin, so quiet, who could possibly want to hurt her? "Did he hit you?"

Silence.

"And that's why you drank?"

"It's part of it, I'm sure."

"That's not enough?"

"It's not an excuse."

"No," I whisper. "It's not."

Neither of us speaks for a few moments. I try to absorb this new information, this new version of my dad who may have yelled and screamed and cried but never laid a finger on us, despite what he'd grown up seeing.

I shift under my blankets, turning from one side to the other, and as sleep continues to elude me, I feel an old familiar itch. My feet stretch and the temptation to pull back my covers and tiptoe down the stairs almost overwhelms me. But I don't have to.

"Would you sing to me?"

A silent beat.

"Of course, Cal."

And finally, as Puff and Jackie Paper sailed past kings and princes that bowed as they floated by, I fell asleep as Puff lost his friend, lost his bravery, and said goodbye to childhood innocence.

*Listen to a performance
piece inspired by the
events of this chapter.*

I'm standing in the field again.

When did I come back here?

But now I know what to expect, and my eyes search the dark expanse surrounding me. It's night though, almost pitch black, and I squint into the emptiness. There. He's here again, just like before, and I sigh, unsure if I'm relieved or annoyed. But this time he's not smiling and he's not looking at me. He's looking up at the sky. The light that I've grown used to, that has surrounded his form since I first came across him right here in this very field, has shifted. It's above him, a circle of shimmering white against a black sky. A glowing orb that, as I watch, gets smaller and smaller. And my dad isn't just *watching* the orb, he's jumping toward it. With each jump, he reaches his arms above him, stretching his fingers farther, but he can't quite catch the light that was once a part of him.

He looks around for help and sees me watching. "Callie! Help, Callie! Please. Help me." He calls my name over and over, but I don't know what I'm supposed to do. I can't get to the light any easier than he can. I rush toward him. Maybe if I kneel on my hands and knees, he can stand on my back and reach it. He's barely over a hundred pounds, I can hold him. But before I can get to him, the light has already moved farther away, now barely the size of a full moon, blending into the night sky, shifting to sit among the stars.

His arms fall to his sides and he drops to his knees on the ground. He's shaking his head. I drop down next to him. I don't know what he's lost, but it's clear he is grieving.

He looks up at me and stares directly into my eyes. "It's too late."

I don't know what I'm apologizing for, but I whisper into the night, "I'm sorry."

He continues shaking his head and then his shoulders start to shake. His torso convulses forward and then back. I reach out to grab his shoulders, to calm his vibrating body, but my hands slide right through him.

"What is it?" I ask. "What's happening?"

But he doesn't hear me because he's still calling my name as his body contorts. "Callie! Help, Callie!"

I blink and the field is gone.

Now it's not him calling my name. It's my mom. I spin around and I'm standing at the top of the stairs in my house. It's still night and my mom is screaming my name, terror lining her voice.

I shake my head and start down the stairs, calling to Taylor over my shoulder. Doesn't he hear her?

I'm across the living room in a second and as I burst into her bedroom, everything is wrong. My dad is on the bed, curled up into a ball, and then stretched out, folding and unfolding violently, shaking, vibrating. My mom is beside him, trying to hold his head. There is blood splattered across his white pillow.

"Callie, call 911!"

I run to the phone even though I know this isn't right. My dad is gone. This already happened. This night *was* real, but we escaped these episodes and this terror. Somehow my shaking fingers hit the right buttons and I am connected with an operator. I try to tell them what's happening, that I think he's having a seizure.

"Why?" they ask.

"He's an alcoholic," I answer.

"Why?" They ask again. *Why?* Why does it matter?

"I don't know . . . but you need to help him."

"Why?"

"Because he needs help!" I scream into the phone.

Why are they asking me this? They're supposed to help. They can't help if they do nothing; if they just stand around asking why, nothing will change.

Finally they say they're on their way.

I tell them my address. Yes, I can wait outside, but I can't imagine they'll have a hard time finding it—the ambulance base is just down the street. Please hurry. Please help him.

I wait in the middle of the road. They're taking too long. I can see the driveway to the station from where I am standing. The darkness presses in around me with each second I don't see head-lights. What are they doing? And then I hear it. The whine of the ambulance. But it doesn't sound like an ambulance. It sounds like a voice, someone calling my name, screaming my name. "Caaaalllliiieee! Caaalllllliieee!"

It's him *and* it's her. It's my mom and my dad *and* it's a wail of an ambulance *and* it's my own voice? "Heeeelllllp, Caaaallllliee!"

I cover my ears. "No!"

I shoot up in bed. It's daylight and I'm in my room, but someone is still calling my name. "Cal-lie!"

"It's okay, Cal." A voice from the edge of my bed.

I jump. He is leaning over me, his hand paused just above my forehead like he wants to push back my sweaty hair or cool my burning skin. But of course, he can't. "It's me. It's just me. Your mom is calling you."

"Callie, are you up? I'm making breakfast."

"I'm up!" My voice is shaking. I'm drenched in sweat. "It was the night of your really bad seizure," I whisper, my hand on my chest.

He sighs. "I'm sorry you went through that."

I don't know how to respond. Me too? I don't say anything. I swing my legs over the edge of the bed and stand up. I go to the bathroom and close the door, trying to provide myself with at least the illusion of privacy. I lean over the sink and splash cold water on my face, washing away the sweat and what I suspect were some tears, but not the lingering remains of the dream. I can't shake the terror of that night even though it's over, even though we've put that time behind us. And why was he so worried about that light disappearing?

I dry my face and shake my head. I can't keep living like this. I step out into the hall and my mom is back at the bottom of the stairs.

She's extending a cup of coffee. "Do you want breakfast?"

I take the mug but shake my head. I'm not even a little hungry. "Not right now. I think I'm gonna work on my speech for a bit."

She nods. "Okay, I'll save you something."

I go back into my room and close the door. I stop to look at him. The light surrounding him, the light he was chasing in my dream, it's . . . smaller? I'd suspected it was changing yesterday, shrinking around him, but today I am certain. Now it's more of an oval, less of a circle. And it's thin, almost as thin as him.

"Everything okay?" he asks.

I shake my head. "'Okay' is relative at this point, I think." I grab the box of his stuff and set it on my bed, sitting down next to it. "It's been real hanging out with a ghost and all, but I think it's time to get you out of here."

"So what's your plan?"

"I'll keep digging through this box and see if it helps me discover some nice stuff I can say at the memorial. I'll give a sweet speech, we'll all get closure, and boom, I won't need to call the Ghost-busters."

"So who *are* you gonna call?" he asks.

"I don't—" I'm not sure how to reply at first and then I see his smirk, and when I catch his eye, he winks. "Clever." I roll my eyes.

"Thank you. But, I actually don't know if that box is going to help."

"What is it?" I ask as I pull out a notebook. I plop down onto my bed, tucking my feet under the blanket, and flip open the book.

He doesn't answer because it's immediately ob-vious that it's a journal. The date is 1988 and the first line reveals it was written during one of his many stays in a rehab facility.

1988. He fought for *so* long.

"I think it's notes, some exercises from rehab. We had to dig pretty deep, Cal, get really honest. I don't know if you want to read . . ."

But I'm already reading.

As I recall, I got drunk 3 or 4 times between the ages of 15 to 20. My actual drinking began when

I started to play music in nightclubs, hotels, and restaurants. I drank for many years without any problems.

In 1976, I met my wife-to-be, so I stopped singing on the road, stayed in more local places . . . now my drinking started to increase.

In 1985 I was arrested for drunk driving and then came my first rehab.

For some reason I always assumed that when my parents first got married, everything was great. Maybe they had some really good years before the drinking got worse and things started to deteriorate. I'd pictured them laughing together, my mom watching him from the audience as he performed, the two of them leaving his shows hand in hand. But as I read and dig and skim, that picture begins to fade and is replaced with another—with the truth.

The dates shock me. I realize I have never had a sober father. He's been this way my entire life. It's no wonder I have such a hard time finding happy memories.

At first, drugs or drinking gave me thrills, bravery, the ability to fit in anywhere. It gave me a boost to create, to perform, to relax. Now drinking just poisons me in all emotional, mental, and physical ways. It changes my personality into someone else. Someone not very pleasant, certainly not happy in any way.

I miss my wife and kids very much and have already learned what I was doing to the family and not realizing the damage. Thank God the babies are small but it will take Bev time to trust again.

I scoff.

I was lonely and felt empty because I couldn't let anyone see inside the prison of shame and guilt I lived in. I thought I was giving my wife and children all my love but in reality, I didn't know how. I despised myself and really didn't understand why.

I loved my wife's father but I didn't know how to show it. I felt cheated and ashamed when he died because I loved him more than my own father. He treated me like one of his own sons, he was a good, kind man. My own father is more worried than he shows but it comes out in anger at my weakness and stupidity.

I don't think I ever let anyone, including my wife, see the real me for fear she would realize what a mistake she had made and leave. I couldn't have taken that kind of pain and rejection. So I lived a false life, showing people what I thought they wanted to see.

Did anyone *ever* really know my father? Did my mom? Maybe the man that came out when he drank was the real him—how would anyone ever know?

They could always tell when I started drinking again. I'd lie of course, try to hide the drinking and what was going on inside me. Eventually I'd overdo it and a different Ed would come home. Terrible words of hate came out of me and they thought they were directed at them, that's the way it sounded, but they were really meant for me. What could I do? I was caught red-handed and of course, the best defense is an offense, especially coming from a drunken mind. Soon the real me was almost gone.

This time I can't let anyone or anything distract me from the road to recovery. I've turned my will all the way over to God. I can't slip into my old ways of thinking, they only lead to pain and suffering for me and those close to me. I must learn to accept the things I cannot change.

I glance up at him. It was the eighties and he was sure he was going to get better. He promised himself he'd get better. He won't look me in the eye and I don't blame him. I go back to reading.

I almost hurt my little girl in an accident. I didn't have her baby seat buckled in properly. I had been smoking and drinking and went to pass a car. I always said the driver never turned her turn signal on but I really don't know . . . we jumped a curb, wrecked the under part of the car and Callie's seat slammed into the dashboard. She didn't get hurt, thank God.

My head shoots up. "You drove drunk with me in the car?"

I am stricken. I feel betrayed, deceived. But if I feel like I've been punched in the stomach, it's nothing compared to how he looks. His mouth is hanging open, and if it's possible for a ghost to go pale, he has.

"It was a—"

"If you say 'mistake,' I'll scream. I knew things were bad, I really did. But the one thing that always comforted me, that told me you weren't like the other drunk dads in movies that hit their kids or did violent, stupid things, was that I *knew* you would never hurt us. No matter what you did, or what demons you were fighting, you loved us and would never put us in danger. At least I *thought* I knew that."

"Cal—"

"No. I can't believe anything you say. These words, '*this time I can't let anyone or anything distract me from the road to recovery,*' they mean nothing. You ignored every good thing you had, you risked it all, you threw your life away, you risked *my* life, for what? A drink? Quick relief? To be numb? Numb to what?"

"You have to understand, it wasn't me. It was a disease."

"A disease you treated! So many times! You came out the other side, but you always went back! But I don't understand *why*. Why did you do it? Why weren't we enough?"

"It was my way of hiding, Cal. Of fighting all the things I'd been told my entire life. I wanted to be a performer more than anything, but every time I stepped up to that stage I was afraid, timid. I didn't believe I deserved to succeed."

"Oh, *please!*" I roll my eyes. "There are plenty of people in the world that feel these things, that go through stuff like this, and they don't drink away everything they love."

"I know it doesn't sound like much, but I'm not talking about being self-conscious, or even embarrassed . . ."

"Then what are you talking about, I don't—"

"Shame!" His voice cracks. "I'm talking about real, deep, almost painful *shame*. I was ashamed of everything I was, and every time I did something wrong, it just confirmed it. Drinking was the only thing that helped me hide from that, even though it made me do the things I was ashamed of. I drank to hide and then I was ashamed of the way I acted so I drank to hide from that shame. It was a cycle I didn't know how to break, and even if I did, I don't know if I would have, because living with that shame . . ." He shakes his head. "I know you can't understand any of this and I'm so glad you can't."

I'm staring down at the bed, refusing to make eye contact. My chest is rising and falling but the rest of me is frozen. "These all sound like excuses. I'm sorry Grandpa was an asshole, I'm sorry you lost people you got close to, but *everyone* goes through this stuff. You could have gotten better, you could have *been* better. You just didn't want to." I lift my gaze and finally look him dead in the eye. "You were weak."

He takes a step back as though he's been pushed, and now it's my turn to feel shame.

A fire starts, not in my belly, but on my neck, creeping up into my cheeks and licking at my forehead, simultaneously moving down and across my chest. I feel rather than see bright red splotches paint across my skin, like one of the abstract paintings of my dad's I'd seen in the basement. I feel a little sick.

I could fix this. Right now. I could tell him I'm sorry and I didn't mean it and release myself from this hot, vicelike grip now squeezing my chest. But shame, as I've just learned, is strong, and cunning, and tricky. It tells you the best way to escape it is to hide from it, or double down. So I do. I ball my hands into fists and lift my chin.

"You said I should tell the truth. That maybe by telling the truth you would go back to where you came from and leave me alone." I stand up and have to fight through a wave of nausea. "So there you go, that's the truth. That's how I really feel. Now, are you going to go?"

He doesn't say anything. He looks up from under the shock of black hair shooting out over his forehead. He blinks slowly, just once, then meets my gaze and holds it. I don't look away. I don't back down. I bite my bottom lip to keep it from quivering. Finally, he nods. One slow, simple movement. And then he drops his chin, closes his eyes, and is gone.

As quickly as he appeared, he is gone and I am left alone.

I grab his journal off the bed and throw it at my wall.

Chapter Eleven

Twenty minutes later, I'm still alone.

The moment the journal hit the wall, I'd hit the ground, collapsing into a pile on my floor. I held my breath, holding back the sobs that were threatening to break free, and waited. I couldn't believe it was over. That after everything, that was all it took to get him to go.

But he's gone.

He doesn't reappear while I sit, still and stone-faced on the floor, staring at the space where he'd just stood.

He doesn't reappear when Stormy comes into the room and pads toward that same spot. She circles the space he'd just filled, looks up into the emptiness, and meows.

"He's gone," I whisper. "C'mere." I snap my fingers to call her over, to comfort her through her loss, but she just stares at me ruefully, lifts her butt into the air for a stretch, and then sprawls out on the floor. "Fine. Be that way."

He doesn't reappear as I stand, stretching out my stiff muscles, and move to my desk.

Stormy's purr turns to an irritated grumble as she dashes out of my way—even though I'm not anywhere near touching her—moves to the bed, and jumps up. She's still gazing at nothing, now to her right, as she settles onto her back paws. She must be looking for him, waiting for him to appear next to her. She'd get used to his absence. We all had to. I sit down and stare at the red words scrawled across the lined paper sitting atop my desk—*"Devoid of feeling."* It's exactly how I feel now.

I wait for the relief that should have come with his departure.

I pick up a pencil and hold it over a fresh sheet of paper. I wait for a new wave of calm, a release of tension, a blanket of solace, any of the emotions I expected would overtake me once I was free of my ghost and released from my past.

But it does not come, and he does not reappear.

I stare out into the late morning, and wonder how many times I'd sat writing by this very window, my hand aching as I tried to keep up with the flow of words straining to get out. And now? There's nothing. I don't feel sick anymore, my neck doesn't feel hot, and I don't feel like I want to cry. I feel nothing and my hand does nothing.

But I guess even back then I didn't write about him. I wrote about teenagers living blissfully sim-ple lives. They had boy trouble and family drama, but nothing like what I was going through. My journal entries are filled with details about crushes and TV shows that I liked (or was obsessed with) and all the things I didn't want to do, but never with him. I never mention his long stints in rehab or visiting him in hospitals. I never rehash his nightly rants or explore my fear or anger. Even when he died, there's nothing. There's no record of that day, what I felt when I heard the news, or details of the days just after. There are no pained realizations or arguments or bargaining with a higher power. I kept my feelings, the anger, the confusion, the guilt, the raw hurt, the questions, and the constant struggle hidden from everyone, even myself. It's no wonder none of it will come out now, no wonder I am *devoid of feeling*.

I don't know how long I sit like that, searching for words that will not come, waiting for a feeling that will not emerge, but it must be long enough to arise suspicion, because eventually I hear footsteps on the stairs and then in the hall, before my mom's face peers around the corner of my door.

"Still working?" she asks. I don't answer.

He doesn't reappear when she—the wife he loved but could never give the type of love she needed—steps into my room. He doesn't reappear when

I turn in my chair to face her, a decision already on my lips.

"If you need food now," she says, "you're going to have to clean it all up because I—"

"I can't speak at the memorial."

She stops talking and steps farther into my room, sitting down on the edge of the bed.

"I thought I could, but I can't. I'm sorry."

I wait for the scolding, for the raised voice or an argument, but none of it comes. She clasps her hands together and sets them on her lap, staring down at them.

"That's it?" she asks softly. "You're just giving up?"

"You're weak." I hear the words I spit at my dead dad echoing in her accusation.

"I'm not giving up." In fact, I'd already achieved the thing I'd set out to do, but she doesn't know that. "It's just not something I feel like I can do right now." She lifts her gaze from her hands to meet mine, but her face remains stoic. She's not getting mad, but I am. "I don't think I should have to explain myself. I don't see why we're even having this memorial in the first—"

"It's for *you,* Callie!"

I jump at the sudden sharpness in her tone. Her voice is still even, calm, but there's a desperation under it that makes me jerk back. She's not yelling—my mom rarely yells and even less so with my dad gone—and she doesn't get mad very often. But she gets hurt. And she's hurt now.

"What do you mean *for me?*" I thought I'd made it pretty clear I didn't want this, any of it. I didn't want the memorial, I didn't want to talk about him or see his family, I just wanted to move on.

Stormy settles down next to her, and my mom sighs like she's told a secret she hadn't meant to spill, but now that it was out there was no holding back.

She shakes her head. "I mean, obviously it's for all of us. It's for him, too. We all need it. But you seem like you really need it. You haven't seemed . . . *well,* over the last year, Callie." She sighs again. "I don't know, maybe this wasn't the right choice."

"I'm fi—"

"You keep *saying* you're fine, but you never come home. When you do, it looks like you've barely slept and you clearly have nightmares. I hear you at night and I hear you mumbling to yourself during the day. You won't talk to me about it. You barely talk to me at all."

My mom and I were close, but we weren't a "spill your emotional baggage" type of family. I knew she was there if I needed her, but I didn't need to talk about this. I needed this whole thing to be over.

"So you're putting on a memorial because I won't talk about my feelings?"

She ignores the sarcasm. "I know you're mad."

I uncross my arms and try to relax my shoulders.

"And it's okay to be mad, but you can't hold on to that forever." She places a hand on Stormy's head, but just lets it sit there. "Actually, if you're going to be mad at anyone, you should be mad at me."

I blink. "You? Why?"

My mom had never been anything but a light in a dark and scary situation. She was comfort, she was stability, she was consistency.

"I'm the one that let him stay. I was an enabler, I know that now. I made some poor choices. I should have kicked him out. I shouldn't have exposed you two to his behavior or let him stay in this house. If I hadn't, maybe—"

"If you hadn't, he could have ended up on the street." I remember the man on the park bench, the bottles in his cart and at his feet, and what he'd said. *"Family doesn't want me around . . ."* I shake my head over and over. No. Seeing him like that, knowing he was out there, unsure where his next meal would come from, *alone*—the thought makes my stomach turn. *That* wasn't what I wanted. "You did what you thought was right and that . . . that spared us from a lot. Please know . . ." I wait until she pulls her gaze away from Stormy and looks at me. "I am *not* mad at you. You were—you *are*—a great mom."

She offers a small smile, but I'm not sure she's fully accepted what I've told her.

"And your dad . . . he . . . ," she tries.

"*He* was barely a dad."

She shakes her head. "He was sick, Callie. Alcoholism is a sickness."

"I *know* that, but it doesn't magically make things better." There were ways to treat illnesses; he just never seemed to want to stick with the treatments.

"He loved you. Both of you . . . so much." Her voice cracks, and I have to swallow down a lump in my throat and blink back a stinging heat in my eyes.

"I know," I whisper.

"He just . . ."

"He just *what?*" I ask. "Didn't love us enough?"

"No." Her tone is sharp again. "Don't think that, don't *ever* think that. He just . . . It's complicated. He was complicated."

I scoff without meaning to. There were things I knew deep down, yes. I knew he loved us. I never really doubted that. I knew alcoholism was a sickness. And sure, I even knew that things were probably more complicated than they seemed, but that didn't make it better. That didn't erase his actions. It didn't erase the fact that if he'd tried a little more, fought a little harder, things would be very different right now.

"There are things you need to understand and accept. We can't change what happened, we can't control it. But we can control what we let control us." Her voice is softer now. "If you don't . . . if you hold onto all of this anger and resentment . . ." She doesn't finish her sentence, just shakes her head.

"Well, I don't know how speaking at a memorial is going to help me let go of anger and resentment, especially when I'm not sure I can think of any-thing nice to say."

"Callie, that can't be—"

"True? It can't be true that I can't think of nice things to say about my drunk of a dad? *Shocking!*"

"Callie, that's enough. If you don't want to speak, fine. If you don't want to have the memorial, fine. But I won't let you sit here and talk about him like that. I would love to have a conversation about the things you're feeling when you're ready, but *this* isn't fair."

"Wait. What did you say?"

She sighs. "We won't have the memorial. I won't make you do anything you don't want to do. It's off."

She stands up and walks out of my room. We're done talking.

Chapter Twelve

Climbed back in the bottle, thought I'd settle the score.

E.S.

I 've won but it doesn't feel like it. I lean back in my chair, watching Stormy settle into the spot my mom just vacated. She doesn't seem to understand that I've won either as she glares at me from the bed, one paw crossed daintily over the other, her judgy eyes darting from me to the doorway. It's like she's trying to tell me something, and I choose to listen to her.

I don't have to be here anymore.

The memorial is off. I can do what I've wanted to do all week—head back to school and finally be left alone. I stand up and begin to pack.

Luckily, most of my clothes are on the floor and have not yet fallen victim to the "company-is-coming cleaning spree" that would surely have possessed my mom if we'd moved a few hours closer to the memorial and the arrival of my grandparents.

As I toss socks and sweatshirts into my bag, a flash of yellow catches my eye, and I see a piece of paper on my floor, one I must have dropped in my haste to grab the notebook and start reading. There are more dates scribbled on the bottom, just like the fake obituary, but these are much later, the ages of his surviving family much older.

I pick up the paper.

Today, I am here to speak about my departed friend Ed. He was a good and kind man. A good father, husband, and friend.

Like most of us, he had his problems, and like most of us, he was able to overcome them. But unlike most of us, his fight was with alcoholism.

There were many times his friends and fami-
ly could hardly take any more. We thought he
had given up because no matter how we tried to
help, he would go back to drinking. And then, Ed
sought help one more time.

Soon he was able to face his problems without
alcohol and without fear. He began to love and
be loved. He became part of our lives, a good
part. His children grew up really knowing their
father, better than they ever dreamed and they
learned that even some of the hardest problems
life has to offer can be overcome.

He found the strength to use the many talents
he'd been wasting to help others and himself. He
reached out to help the ones who suffered and
gave them hope and found peace. He became the
person he was always meant to be. He never be-
came a singing star—instead he became whole.

My throat is clogged and tears stream freely
down my face. He would never become this man he
so desperately wanted to be. His children never got

to know him, he never got to help others, he never found peace and he never became whole.

I press my lips together to hold back a sob. But *why?* Why couldn't he find those things, *be* those things?

I throw the paper back to the ground and stand up.

I can't be in this house anymore. I need to breathe.

I am down the hall and downstairs so fast it's like it's Christmas morning.

I move through the living room and toward the front door, but Taylor is there, blocking my path.

"What's going on?" he asks. "I thought I heard yelling earlier and now Ma won't come out of her room."

"The memorial is off." I try to push past him, but he steps in front of me.

"What?"

I shrug. "It's off. Mom is canceling it."

"Why, because you threw a fit?"

I wince. "I didn't throw a— What's the big deal anyway?"

"Just because you didn't want it doesn't mean I didn't."

"You said you barely think about him!"

"That doesn't mean I don't miss him. Both things can be true. And Mom was right. I was too shocked and overwhelmed at the funeral to really accept it, to take it all in and say goodbye. It would have been nice to have one more chance."

I stand there with my mouth hanging open. My chest is getting hot again and the fingers of shame are crawling up my neck and cheeks. I have to get out of here.

Before I can decide how to respond or push past him toward the door, my phone buzzes.

Taylor watches me as I pull it from my pocket.

It's a message in a group text of kids from high school. It's only active during holidays or breaks when some of us might be home.

"Party tonight at the firepit."

I hesitate, my thumbs hovering over the keys on my phone. I start moving toward the *n* to reject the invitation but something stops me.

Why shouldn't I? The memorial is off. Everyone in my house is mad at me and there's nothing waiting for me at school except a poorly written project that's only going to make me doubt my abilities as a writer and, in turn, my entire identity. A night off from the freak show that is my life would do me good.

"Callie . . ." Taylor speaks slowly as though he's afraid to scare me. He's right to think I might be a little jumpy, which is exactly why I need to relax.

I lift my eyebrows. "Are we done here?"

"Who is that?"

"None of your business." He's only asking to get me to say it. He can see my screen and he knows I know it.

"You probably shouldn't—"

"Last I checked you don't get to tell me what to do."

He throws his hands up. "Fine. Do whatever you want. See if I care."

"I will." I push past him. Grabbing my keys off the table in the sitting room, I head out the door.

I add my car to the row that's already formed on an old friend's property behind their house. The firepit is actually just a big burn pile in the middle of a field. It was a popular place for parties when we were in school, but I never really attended then. So far my eighteen years have been lived out as a relatively well-behaved average student who liked to read and only gave my parents the occasional sarcastic comment. Partying, blurry nights, and sick mornings were only things I heard about but never experienced. My mom had enough to deal with and I'd always known it. Why add to her worries?

But now nothing made sense.

My dad died and everything and nothing made sense all at once.

He died and I was sad and relieved and, yes, a little guilty. Okay, a lot guilty. And pissed. But not as pissed as I was when he came back. I was guilty and pissed and ashamed and for the last few days I'd been *seeing ghosts,* so why not indulge a little? Why not just have a good time?

I didn't want to be the teen who'd just lost a parent. The friend who everyone feels sorry for and whispers about when she walks away. I feel their stares as I approach the bonfire and I know what they are thinking and I am so done with all of it. If he used drinking to escape the shame and powerlessness he'd felt most of his life, why couldn't I?

I step up to the fire and hear surprised voices shouting my name, inviting me into their circle, their rituals. But the heat of the bonfire isn't enough to burn away the constant ache that is always with me or the sting of his reaction as he'd dropped his head at my words, *"You were weak."*

Maybe he was.

The hum of my old classmates isn't enough to erase the words scribbled across my memory—*"He never became a singing star, instead he became whole."*

Except he hadn't.

The concerned glances of my classmates who only remember me as the girl whose dad died are making me dizzy and the plastic bottle is in my hand before I can "just say no."

If my dad drank the cheap stuff and his bottle was always glass, what did that say about this? I wrinkle my nose. The smell should turn me off.

Why did people drink this stuff?

Why did he?

Why had he thrown away everything to chase something that smelled like it was used to clean wounds that had already started to turn on muddy battlefields?

It's time to find out.

I take a sip. Well, more than a sip. If I sipped, I knew I would spit it out and never let the disgusting liquid touch my lips ever again, so I take a swig. And it is awful. I immediately want to vomit and my throat burns and my stomach turns, but the crowd around me cheers and laughs and suddenly I'm not just the girl with the dead dad. I'm not the Goody-Two-Shoes who everyone thought got great grades but was really failing math all through school and now is failing at the one thing she thought she was good at.

Suddenly, I'm a regular college kid who doesn't have to worry about whether one drink will activate some sort of alcoholic gene and send me spiraling toward the bottom of a bottle night after night.

So I ignore the signals my body is sending me, the warning bells that are clanging in my head and the image of him that suddenly seems to be dancing just above the flames of the fire. I turn away from the vision. He's gone, returned to wherever it was he came from, and he still won't leave me alone. I take another swig. With each drink he fades a little, but if I find myself distracted by conversation or laughter and stop sipping (I can sip now because it doesn't taste so terrible), he reappears.

So I motion for the bottle again.

Every time my friends ask, "Callie, are you okay?"

I insist I'm fine and take another drink.

I drink until he stops appearing at the edge of my vision.

I drink until I forget about the last few days.

I drink until I'm not sure where I am.

I drink until it seems I have the ability to move through time. One moment I'm in front of the fire, the next I'm leaning against someone's car.

One moment I'm laughing at a joke, the next I'm grabbing the bottle from someone as I'm urged to "Do another shot!"

One moment I'm being held up by one of the guys from my class, the next I'm dancing to a country song playing from a speaker and I hear, "You're awesome!" from a kid I've barely ever spoken to.

One moment I am fine, and then I am not.

And then I am on the ground.

And then I'm pulled up.

Someone says, "She's had enough."

Someone yells, "She's gonna be sick," and then I'm doubled over and I'm not having any fun and hot tears burn my eyes and my whole face is on fire.

"We have to get her home."

"I can't drive."

"Me neither."

I'm on the ground, my back resting against a car, my knees pulled to my chest as the voices above me try to decide what to do with me. The ground keeps moving up to meet me until my face is pressed against the cold grass, but as soon as I feel myself relax, the world is spinning and I'm being pulled up again. Why won't they let me rest? I need sleep.

And then I am crying.

I can't stop the sobs or the words that come pouring out like the vomit of only moments before. "This isn't me," I sob. "I don't want to be this. I don't want to be like him."

"It's okay," I hear. "He's coming."

"No! He can't come. He's gone now. He left me and I don't want him here." But I do. I do want him here. But he can't be. He's not supposed to be here, because he died and I am so, so sad that he died.

I don't know how much time passes.

At one point, I lay down in the grass again and sob. This time no one pulls me back up.

And then there is nothing. So much nothing. And it's wonderful. There's no dead dad, and no party, and no failing grades and no memorial.

But there is *something*. Something lurking in the blackness, and as I try to find it or avoid it, I get dizzy and my stomach threatens to turn on me again.

When I open my eyes, I am moving and my body is screaming at me to stop, to stay still. I try to speak, "No . . . stop."

"We're going home, Callie."

I try to blink, try to bring the figure beside me into focus. It can't be him.

"This isn't me," I repeat emphatically, pathetically. I have to say it over and over again. I have to reassure everyone, I have to reassure myself.

"I know, you've said."

He kind of sounds like him. I squint—he has his nose.

But he's gripping the steering wheel and pressing his foot into the gas pedal so it can't be him. I see him clearly now and I immediately close my eyes again, shame washing over me as he cranks his window down. "Don't you dare throw up."

"You can't drive yet," I whisper.

"I have my permit, and you're a licensed driver."

He shouldn't have to do this. We escaped this. When he died, we at least had that. We'd never have to pick him up from a bar and carry him home after a night out, or drag him kicking and screaming from a party. When he died, he released us from that future. And then I pulled us back in.

Another sob escapes my throat. The alcohol has dissolved my shields, roared like a tidal wave over the dam I'd built around that part of my heart.

"I'm sorry," I sob.

He doesn't say anything.

"I never wanted this. I don't want to be like him."

My brother takes his eyes off the road briefly, sparing me a quick, pitying glance. "You don't have to be."

Chapter Thirteen

*If this be the last chance for us, don't
stand asking why.*

E.S.

I wake up in my bed.

This is another nightmare, I think as I try
to lift my head off my pillow, my consciousness
swimming through a hangover haze and struggling to separate reality from impossibility. I don't
know what's real anymore. I expect to see my dad
standing at the edge of my bed, but I don't know
why. He's been dead for a year. I expect to be back
in my bed in my dorm at school, but I am home, and
I don't know if the last few days have been a dream
or if last night was the dream or if—

I jump as I blink my eyes open. There is someone on my bed with me, but it's not my dad.

"You! What the h—?" I try to sit up but immediately fall back onto my pillow.

"I'm sorry," says Harley, the psychic living in my grandparents' old farmhouse, "I didn't mean to scare you."

"How . . . *why?*" I want to know what she's doing in my house, but I can't form full sentences. My head feels like it's being ripped off my shoulders and the room is spinning.

"I had to come see you. I just . . . I felt like something was wrong."

I groan. I can't even get out a sarcastic response, and that hurts more than my head, for at least a second.

"I tried to knock but no one answered and the door was open. Ya'll don't lock your doors?"

I moan in response.

She lifts her hands. "Sorry, sorry."

I whisper past the cotton ball in my mouth. "You *felt* like something was wrong?"

"Well, clearly I was right. Are you okay? Can I get you anything? Water?"

I try to shake my head but can't manage it. Instead I motion toward the box on the floor. She looks over and sees what it is.

"Ah. I see."

"Why?" I whisper. It's not everything I want to say, but it's all I can get out.

"It belonged to your dad, I thought—"

I wave my hand to stop her. "Did you read any of it?"

She shakes her head. "Of course not."

"But you knew what it was? Or, had a 'sense'?" I find the strength to make air quotes with my fingers and she lifts an eyebrow.

"Yes, I had a sense."

"Why would we want those things? Why would I want to know those things?"

"I didn't know *exactly* what was in it, Callie. It just felt like it held . . . important truths. It's the details of our past that make us who we are. Sometimes you need to step back and review the details to get the big picture."

She was speaking in riddles again and it made my head spin even more. I push a hand to my eyes.

"Well, it doesn't matter anymore," I mumble through dry lips.

"What do you mean?"

"The memorial is canceled and he's gone. I spoke my truth, I guess."

"He's gone? As in crossed back?"

"I guess. I yelled at him, he sort of 'poofed' away, and I haven't seen him since."

"Are you sure he's gone?"

I peel my eyes open into half a squint. Why was she questioning this? "Yeah, can't you tell?"

"I should be able to, yes. But I still sense the same presence I did the day you left the field and the day you stopped to visit. Can't you?"

I can barely sense anything beyond the pounding in my head and the angry churning in my stomach.

"I don't know. You're the medium, not me." But even as I say it, something catches my eye to her right. It's like someone has poked at the air around us, and like a river's surface that's been broken by a pebble, there is a ripple and a shimmer of light. I realize I don't feel any different than I did when he was sitting on my bed next to me, or than I did when he was in the car with me. I don't feel as empty as I did a few days ago in that field before he showed up.

"Oh."

She sighs. "I was afraid of this."

"Afraid of what?"

"He's still here, Callie. And you're almost out of time."

"Out of . . . What do you mean he's still *here?*" I already know she's right, but I don't understand what's happening.

"He didn't cross back. He must be hiding from you. And you're wasting valuable time."

"Why do you keep saying that? What do you mean?"

"If he doesn't cross back over soon, he could be trapped here."

"Tra— What? I don't—"

"You don't know." She looks around as though trying to confirm something. "He never told you." It wasn't a question.

"Told me what?" I demand, shifting myself up to rest on one arm. I press my lips together and hold my breath, waiting for the room and her words to come into focus.

"Once your father crossed onto our plane, a clock started ticking."

I stare.

"He's already crossed over once. He's not meant to be *here*. The longer he stays, the less likely it is he'll be able to return. If he's here too long . . ."

"If he's here too long, *what?*"

"He won't be able to get back. He'll be stuck here."

"Here? Like . . . with me? He will be here, with me, following me around . . . *forever?*"

She tilts her head. "It's more than that, Callie. If he's caught here, he will never be at rest. He'll be lost between two worlds, never truly a part of either."

Before I can stop them, the words spoken the day of his funeral whisper through my ears like a breeze. *"And now, he is at peace."* And I feel the collective sigh of relief that went through his family. *Finally.* Finally he was at peace. *Was.* And now he isn't.

I look to the spot where I'd seen the shimmer in the air, the spot where Stormy is currently circling. The stupid cat had known the whole time.

Harley is watching Stormy as well. "Animals are very perceptive about these things."

I ignore her. "Is she right? Are you still here?"

And then, just like in the field, he's back in front of me. His head is bowed and he doesn't greet me or say anything. Stormy meows.

"You knew about this."

He doesn't reply, and I know what he isn't saying.

"And *you* knew about this." I look back at Harley. "You were trying to tell me, at your house."

"He didn't want me to. I could tell he wanted to be the one, but . . . he never did."

I turn back to him. "But *why*? Why did you come back in the first place?"

He looks up. "You were hurting."

"But . . . you were *free*. From all of it. From the pain, from the memories of your dad, from the shame. It was over. You were at peace."

"But *you* weren't. I couldn't leave you like that, Cal."

I have so many questions, almost too many to form in my current state. Between the hangover and this new information and his reappearance, my brain feels like it's short-circuiting. "But you knew. You knew there was a time limit?"

"I . . . It wasn't spelled out for me or anything, but I had a feeling. Somehow I felt my time would be limited if I came back, yes."

"And you knew the consequences."

He shrugs his assent.

"But you came back anyway."

"Yes."

"And you didn't tell me."

"Your whole life has been spent worrying about me and my problems. I wanted to do this for you. You needed me."

I fall back onto the bed, bringing my hands to my face, and moan. He moves forward, reaching out like he wants to touch me, comfort me, but he can't.

"Callie," Harley says softly from beside me, placing a hand gently on my shoulder, "what are you thinking?"

What am I thinking? I don't even want to admit to myself what I'm thinking. My dad just admitted he'd risked an eternity of peace to help me, and all I can think is . . . *It isn't fair.* I didn't ask him to come back. I'd gone to that field to get something off my chest, and the second he'd shown up, he'd ruined it, and now, instead of doing my best to get back to my life, I had to . . . *what?* Get him back where he belonged or he'd be a trapped spirit forever? I'd just wanted a good night's sleep and had somehow stumbled into a ghost-hunting reality show.

But I wasn't going to say any of that to this woman. She wasn't my shrink . . . but maybe she could help.

"So, I have to send him back. How? What do I do?"

"Well, you brought him here. He came back for you, so sending him back is also up to you."

Why did everyone keep saying that to me? "Fantastic. What am I supposed to do? We're not having the memorial tomorrow. I thought he was gone. He wanted me to think he was gone."

I look to each of them, a ghost no one else can see to my right and a psychic medium who broke into my house, sitting next to me on my bed as I lie feeling like I'm about to die. *What is my life?* "How much time is left?"

"That, I don't know. I would imagine not much. His energy, his presence is much stronger than it was the other day. His connection to the other side is fading and his connection to this world is growing."

Maybe *she* couldn't tell me, but when I looked at him, I saw the light that had followed him around since his appearance. It was something that was just a part of him, something I was used to now, but then I remembered my dream and his desperation to reach the light. It was his connection to the other side, his door to peace, and it was fading, closing.

I sigh.

"You're mad," says Harley.

"That my dad is haunting me and might be stuck as my shadow forever? Yeah, I'm a little mad."

"At your dad. You've been mad at him for a long time."

"And my anger is keeping him here and I need to let it go and what, forgive him? Tell him how much I love him? After all I've been through, all that's happened, now I have to . . . what? Give *him* the peace I haven't even been able to—"

"No, Callie."

I stop talking and open my eyes, his tone startling me out of my rant. I feel like he's scolded me for touching something I shouldn't have. His usually soft, low voice is sharp. A high note on a piano accidentally bumped while trying to settle onto the right key.

"I don't expect any of that from you. Maybe . . ." He sighs, looking defeated for the first time since appearing before me in the field. "Maybe this is what I deserve."

My stomach clenches. I suck in a breath, which is a huge mistake.

The sudden expansion of my stomach and rush of oxygen to my brain make everything spin, and I suddenly don't care who is in my house, I'm going to vomit.

"I'm gonna be sick."

Harley jumps up and I throw my legs over the bed. Reaching for anything I can grab to steady me on my way, I rush to the bathroom just outside my room and slam the door behind me.

As I reexperience the taste and smells of the evening I can barely remember, I'm suddenly certain this is not the first time I've been sick in the last twelve hours, and a rush of shame makes my cheeks hot and I gag again at the thought. My throat burns and tears stream down my cheeks. How did people do this again and again, night after night . . . some for an entire lifetime?

I flush the toilet and fall back, leaning against the bathtub, the tile of the bath and floor cool against my burning body. My stomach isn't churning, but I don't feel relieved.

There is a knock on the door and then Harley's voice. "Callie, I should go."

I want to say "duh," but I'm afraid to open my mouth. "Mmm-hmm," I hum around pursed lips.

"Callie, just . . . just remember how much is at stake here."

Like I could forget.

I hear her retreating footsteps in the hall and then I jump.

He's standing near my shoulder, and the sudden movement from the scare throws a sharp pain up through my neck and into my head and I groan. My dead dad is still haunting me, and now I have a pounding head, parched mouth, and the dim recollection of an embarrassing night to contend with, along with what might actually be a complete mental and emotional collapse.

I drop my head to my knees and close my eyes.

Everything hurts—and I mean everything. Yes, my body feels as though it's been run through a wood chipper, but my insides throb too. My chest aches as I remember the words that made me run to the party in the first place—my own, terrible accusation, *"You could have been better. You're weak."*

And then the party. The calls and the shouts and the cheers and the concern and the crying . . . oh, the crying.

And, of course the constant nagging and wondering, *Am I turning into him?*

And now it's over, but it isn't.

There is still a burning in my stomach, guilt pressing into my chest, and a pounding.

After a few long minutes of aching silence, I look up again. He's still there and he's smiling, though I can't imagine why. Maybe he's happy I'll be joining him on the other side soon, because this constant pounding in my head is clearly going to kill me. I wince.

No, now it's not just my head that is pounding. There's a banging on the bathroom door and I cringe.

"Callie! What are you doing? It's almost noon."

My mom. I groan in response. That's all I can manage.

"Are you okay?"

"Mmmmm-hmmm."

"Well, hurry up and come downstairs. We're waiting."

We?

I hear her footsteps in the hall and then on the stairs.

I push myself up cautiously and move as quietly as I can out into the hall, back into my bedroom, and collapse onto my bed. My pillow actually feels like steel. I need water, but I can't go down there.

"She knows. You know that, right?"

I grunt. I know she knows, but I am happier pretending I don't.

"Who is 'we'?" I ask, pressing my hands to my eyes and trying not to talk too loudly.

"Your grandparents."

I sit up, but it's too fast too soon. "Ohhh, no." I immediately fall back down, the room still spinning even as I settle back onto the bed. "I think I'm still drunk."

I hear a low chuckle and my eyes shoot open. Is he laughing at me?

"I'm sorry," he says, lifting his hands. "It's just, I know the feeling well."

"Well, it's new to me."

"I'm glad. And you're not still drunk. If you were, you would not be feeling this awful, trust me."

"This is a really sweet father-daughter lesson, but we have bigger things to deal with. Why are Grandma and Grandpa here?"

"The memorial."

"But the memorial was canceled."

"But their flight wasn't. Your mom probably let them come into town anyway. That's where she was when Harley got here."

"Do *they* know?"

"I think everyone knows."

"Oh god." I pull a pillow over my face and lie there for a moment with pounding temples and a churning pool of hot lava in my stomach. The cool of the pillow feels good on my face. I am drowning and being tossed around in rough seas and lying as still as I possibly can, all at the same time. There is darkness but also a harsh light somewhere behind the black, and even though my eyes are closed, it hurts.

"What happened last night?" He asks it as though we are sitting at the breakfast table having pancakes and orange juice, perusing the newspaper. He asks it as though he had ever been the type of dad to sit at the breakfast table and peruse the newspaper over pancakes and orange juice.

I don't answer. He knows perfectly well what happened.

I pull the pillow off my face and glare at him. Why had he done this to himself over and over? My expression must give away my silent question, because he gives a small head shake and shrugs as if to say, "I wish I had an answer."

We stare at each other for a moment, and I notice how dim the light is behind him. I shift but then wince.

He tilts his head.

"Okay," I say, "we have to figure out how—"

"No," he says. "We don't have to figure out anything. You need to rest, get over this thing."

"This *thing* is my own damn fault." I shake my head and then swallow around another wave of nausea. "I messed everything up—"

Before I can go on, there's another knock on my door.

"Callie?" It's Taylor.

I sigh. I don't know if I'm ready to face him.

"Ma said to let you know everyone is going to lunch."

I could go. I should go. I should brush my teeth and my hair and face my family like a . . . well, like someone braver than me would. But I'm not feeling very brave at the moment.

"Can you tell them I'm sick?" As soon as the words are out of my mouth, I'm afraid I'll actually be sick again. I hate this feeling, I hate what I did, I hate myself.

There's a pause on the other side of the door. I don't know if Taylor will lie for me after what I put him through last night. I definitely don't deserve any favors from him. But after a second there's a quiet "Sure." And then footsteps in the hall, then on the stairs, and then silence.

I let myself fall back onto my bed once more. Maybe I could just stay here all day. I catch movement out of the corner of my eye and am reminded of why I can't. I don't have all day. I don't know how long I have, but I know it's not long.

"Callie," he says softly and I look up. "I can help."

I shake my head. "I'm the one that needs to—"

"I mean with the hangover. You're not going to be able to do anything as long as you feel like this."

I don't respond.

"I do have some experience getting rid of a hangover."

I blow out air through my nose. No kidding.

"If you go to the kitchen, I can tell you what to make. It will help, I promise. And then, from there, we can work out another plan to, well . . ." He shrugs, but I know what he means.

I study him for a moment before I respond. Despite his situation he seems calm, cool even.

He stands over me, his hands in his pockets, as though he's waiting against his car to pick me up after school. Though, he'd never picked me up after school, and if he had he would have stuck out in the parking lot filled with stay-at-home moms and T-ball-coach dads. He was more at home in a smoky bar holding a guitar than in the PTA.

He's right about one thing, though. I probably need something in my stomach. My whole body shudders at the thought, and I can already feel my taste buds recoiling, but my dry mouth at least needs water.

He's already waiting for me in the kitchen by the time I make my way there. I go to the cupboard and grab a glass. I fill it with water and sip as I stand in the light coming from the window above the sink, pondering what might stay in my stomach.

"Do you guys still have tomato juice on hand?" he asks.

I lift my eyebrows. Tomato juice had been one of his favorite drinks. No one else in the house liked it. Was that why *he* liked it? It helped with hangovers?

"It always worked for me."

I set the water on the counter and go to the cupboard. I push some items aside, and in the back I find one lone can that no one has touched for months.

I stare at it skeptically.

"It's either that or pickle juice."

I almost gag and he laughs.

"Actually if you have some, you should add just a splash. And some spices."

For a few minutes, he guides me around the kitchen, telling me what to add to my concoction and assuring me that if I could just keep down the first few sips, it would eventually taste good. If the smell is any indication, I highly doubt it, but if it will get rid of this pounding and put me on steadier feet, I'll try anything. Even something invented by my alcoholic ghost father.

When I'm done, I have a piece of toast with butter and a glass of thick, sludge-like liquid that could clear even my mom's worst sinus infections.

I take my breakfast to the kitchen table and he joins me. I sip my juice and nibble my bread, testing the limits of my stomach. At the moment, I feel like it would probably be fine if I never ate again. I'm definitely entertaining the idea of never drinking again.

"You doing okay?" he asks softly.

I shrug and lift my drink, trying to signal that the question is still up for debate.

"I don't just mean right now. I've had a hangover, I know you'll live. I mean, *how are you doing?*"

My usual answer bounces to my tongue, but maybe it's the booze or the nasty drink that causes it to fizzle and evaporate, because I don't shoot off an "I'm fine." Instead, I pause and really think about the answer for the first time in a very long time.

After a few seconds of thinking and nibbling and sipping, I give the first honest answer I've given in years. "I don't know."

He nods. "You'll be okay eventually, you know? You're strong, like your mom. You'll all be fine."

"But what about you?"

"What about me? I had my chance at fine. I had great right in front of me and I let it slip through my fingers. Like you said, I could have been better."

I shake my head. "I shouldn't have said that." I still don't know exactly how I feel about my dad and our life, his death, or even his haunting, but I know what I said was cruel and I know I didn't mean it.

"It's okay, Cal. I forgive you."

I sigh. Everyone made forgiveness seem so easy.

I take another sip of my drink. It's going down easier, and he was right, it doesn't taste so bad. The room isn't spinning and the Tylenol he insisted I grab from the bathroom is starting to kick in. But my brain still feels slow and fuzzy.

"Can you . . . just talk to me?" I ask.

"Talk to you?"

"Yeah, distract me a little. Tell me some things I don't know."

"Something you don't know . . ." He stares out the window for a second, thinking, and then laughs a little. "When I was little, but old enough to wander around the farm by myself, I made my way to the chicken coop. In the coop, I found some little round brown pellet-looking things that looked a lot like chocolate cookies. So—"

"No!" I gasp, throwing my hand over my mouth. "Don't say it."

"I ate them."

My throat makes a strange noise and I shake my head. "Why would you tell me that right now?"

He's laughing. "Sorry! You said—"

"Tell me something else, *anything* else."

So, he starts talking. While I drink my tomato juice and nurse my first hangover, my dad tells me his stories. And for the first time in my life, or the first time I can actually remember, I listen.

He tells me that he started writing music at six years old while helping his grandpa make deliveries, his face pressed against the glass of the truck, using everything he saw along the road as inspiration. I smile as I remember doing the exact same thing in the back of our car, making up a song about the moon and serenading it as we drove.

He tells me about a horse he was gifted when he was ten named Pinto, and all the productions he was in from elementary school to college and after. He tells me that in the summer of 1968 the papers said he was on his way to becoming one of the nation's top artists but that a motorcycle accident almost caused him to lose his leg and his career. It took three operations to save his leg.

I can picture the scar on his calf from the skin grafts. It was a perfectly smooth square where absolutely no hair grew.

He tells me about the hospital tours he did after that and the letter he received from the governor thanking him for the fine work he was doing.

He told me how much he loved being an entertainer and how good he was at it.

He tells me he was in the navy for two years and about coming in off the road to sing locally when he met my mom. He tells me about their first home, a little trailer on a lake and all the time they spent on their boat and at hotels where he was playing and how much he loved her family and how much more they supported him during his worst times than his own family did.

He tells me so many stories from when my brother and I were little that my head starts to spin again, and I start to think that it's a little unfair that he has those memories and I don't, because by the time I can start to see pictures of my life he's—

I shake my head and choose not to dwell on that.

He tells me about playing with Elvis's band, and his run at the Grand Hotel on Mackinac Island and his record label and his movie offer. He tells me about playing at the Republican National Convention, which I think is funny because he'd always been adamant about not having any political affiliations.

When he stops talking, my drink and toast are gone and my stomach has settled a little. I'm still tired and confused. I no longer have the energy to be angry or even frustrated, but I still don't understand.

"You had a lot going for you."

He nods slowly. "I did."

"You were really talented."

He nods again.

"Did . . ." I'm afraid to ask my next question. It's going to sound awful and I don't want him to "run" away again, but I have to ask. "Did you even try to get better?"

"I did try, Cal. I tried so hard for all of you. For my parents, for my friends. It may not look like it, but I fought. I fought it so hard that . . . well, here I am."

My next question, the one that's been haunting me even longer than the figure in front of me, is replaced with a new one.

"What about for *you*?"

"What?"

"You said you fought for us, for your parents, for everyone else . . . but did you fight for yourself?"

He blinks at me as though no one has ever asked him this question.

"I . . ."

"Weren't *you* worth fighting for?"

He looks down at the table. "I guess I never really thought about it."

"That's really sad," I whisper before I can stop myself. It was meant to be an inside thought, but maybe my synapses were still slow.

He lifts his gaze to mine and gives a small half smile. "Yeah, I guess it is."

I want to ask my next question, I still need answers, and now is probably the best time, sitting here, talking together like we haven't in years . . . but it doesn't seem fair at the moment. He's staring out the window in front of him and I know I should give him a few minutes, but the morning has already shifted into afternoon and his light is fading with every passing second.

"I still don't understand," I whisper, and he looks up. "Why?"

He doesn't have to ask what I mean, and he stares at me for a few seconds before taking a deep breath and opening his mouth. "I—"

I hear the creak of the door and stand up as someone struggles to push the main door open. I force myself to pull away from the answer that never made it past my dad's lips and make it to the doorway of the kitchen as the front door pops open and I hear my mom's voice.

"I'm sure she's up and about now."

My grandpa's deep voice follows as they pile into the house. "Not if she's anything like her father. She'll be up there all day and only come down to ask for money before heading back out to the bar or to a party. She'll waste her life, just like him, mark my words."

"Bill . . ." My grandma tries to interject, but he talks right over her.

"I knew that boy should have never had kids. Wasn't man enough to take care of his own family and now look . . . turning out just like him. It's a vicious cycle."

I step out of the kitchen. I hear my dad call my name from behind me, but I don't stop. I march over to where they're all standing in the center of the sitting room with their coats still on. I'm standing in front of my white-haired, thick, and stocky, yet hunched with age Grandpa and I'm ready to *go*. Who did he think he was? Maybe my dad's actions weren't entirely my grandpa's fault, but he was definitely not innocent in all of this either. He couldn't just brush aside the part he'd played in the fate of his son, and he certainly couldn't talk about him like that. Sure, my dad made mistakes, he wasn't the person he should or could have been, but no matter what he'd done, he didn't deserve to be remembered like this. And he doesn't deserve to be stuck here.

My mouth, already opened to say all of this to my grandpa, snaps shut, and I almost double over as my epiphany punches me in the stomach and all the air leaves my chest.

Oh. Shit.

"Well, Missy," says my grandpa, his white mustache twitching, "I heard you had quite a night."

I am momentarily struck dumb by the realization that has just popped some bubble in my brain. A bubble that has been growing and taking up space and blocking feelings and emotions for years. Now that bubble has burst.

When I don't respond, he continues. "Incredibly irresponsible of you but can't expect much else, I suppose. It's probably good this whole thing is off."

I could respond. I could tell him he can't talk about my dad like that, and if he was so worried about vicious cycles he shouldn't have hit his wife or constantly berated his children, but I don't. Instead I change course and turn to the only one in the room strong enough to help a new generation break those cycles.

"Mom. I'm sorry." I don't say more than that, she knows what I'm sorry for, because the second the words leave my mouth, her shoulders relax and she sighs.

"Oh, Callie, it's—"

But I keep going before I chicken out. "And I want to have the memorial. You were right. We all need it. He *deserves* it." I shoot a look at my grandpa. "Is it too late?"

"No," she says quietly, "it's not too late."

"Okay. I'll go work on my speech. Will you call Harley?"

She nods.

I look around. "Where's Taylor?"

"He went upstairs as soon as we got home." She lowers her voice. "I think he was worried about you. We all were."

It's my turn to nod. "I know. I think I'm okay, though. Or at least"—I glance over my shoulder and catch his eye—"I will be. We all will be." I reach out and wrap my arms around her shoulders. "I love you." Then I turn and hurry, as much as I am able to at least, up the stairs.

I find Taylor in the hall, and I assume he was just checking my room and the bathroom. I hide a smile that would say how sweet I think it is that he's worried and stop in front of him with a small wave.

"Hey."

"Hey."

An emotional sibling reunion.

I don't beat around the bush. "Thank you for coming to get me last night."

He shrugs.

"I'm . . . I'm sorry. About everything. About the memorial and the way I acted. I-I've got a lot on my mind right now."

He shrugs again and I'm beginning to think that might be all I get, when he says, "I know. I get it."

"Yeah," I say, "I know you do. And I'm sorry for forgetting that."

A moment of silence. He stares down at his feet.

"The memorial is back on," I add and he looks up. "Do you still have the music ready to go?"

He nods. "Are you going to speak?"

I glance toward the bottom of the stairs where he is waiting and watching. "I think I have to."

Taylor doesn't know exactly what I mean, but he seems to understand.

"Are you ready?" he asks.

It's my turn to shrug. "I will be."

Chapter Fourteen

Let your voices ring together now, and raise a final cry.

E.S.

I sit at my desk in my room, again. A blank piece of paper sits in front of me, again. The ghost of my dad "sits" on the edge of my bed while I try to write a speech filled with nice things about him in less than twelve hours. These are not ideal writing conditions.

"This has to be it," I say, more to convince myself than him, "I'll say nice things at the memorial and that will help you cross." I turn to look over my shoulder and gauge his reaction. His face doesn't give anything away. "You don't agree?"

"I hope so, Cal."

I sigh. "You could help a little more, ya know. It's your eternity we're talking about here."

"But it's your journey."

I can feel my anger and frustration bubbling to the surface. "I know but—"

"Cal?"

"Yeah?"

"Is this really that hard? Did I really give you so few good memories?" His voice is soft and it cuts me.

"I . . ." I honestly don't know what to say.

I want to think of an argument, memories that don't involve bottles or yelling or long green hallways in rehab centers or broken family vacations. I want to tell him that despite everything, the good outweighs the bad and I want to write all the good down and tell everyone at the memorial how wonderful he was. I *want* to set him free.

I open my mouth and then close it again.

He sighs. "I'm so sorry." It's so quiet, like a whisper on a breeze. "I'll leave you alone to work on this."

Before I can protest, he's gone. Well, not gone, I know that, but not with me, not near me as he has been over the last few days. I don't see a flash of black hair out of the corner of my eye or hear him humming to himself. He's not singing into the darkness as I drift off to sleep or offering up random facts about movies or music. He's not chuckling as he listens to me rant or Taylor and I fight. Without his presence, without him, the room feels very empty and I feel suddenly very, very alone.

And then I start to write.

✳✳✳

I am back on the farm. My last few visits, both in real life and my most recent nightmare, have been stressful and strange, but this time my mom is here and holding my hand and a cold front and covering of clouds has created a cool breeze that blows my hair around my face and I know *this* is real.

My grandpa is grumbling about the cold, and my brother is holding a portable CD player with my dad's song "Run for Your Brother" queued up and ready to go. Chuck and Manny are smiling at me from across the small circle of loved ones that have gathered and I try to smile back. But I am distracted. I haven't seen my dad since he disappeared when I was working on my speech.

I try not to think about the paper trembling in my hand. The paper I will be expected to read from in just a few moments and everything riding on the words scribbled across it. They weren't the words I thought I would write. I'm not even sure they are the right ones. But they were the first things I thought when I realized just how alone I felt in my bedroom when my dad blipped away.

Instead, I try to focus on not throwing up. I'm not hungover anymore, but I still feel sick.

My mom squeezes my hand and steps into the center of the circle. She thanks everyone for coming. She repeats a lot of the same sentiments I imagine were shared at the funeral, but it turns out she was right—I don't remember a whole lot from that day, and today those sentiments hit harder.

"I know we all had a lot of hard times with Ed," she says, looking around the circle because every single person in the circle did, "but I hope we can all put those in the past and remember the good times." She turns to look at Taylor and me. "We must always remember, your dad is at peace now." My stomach twists. "I hope he is smoking a cigar with my dad, and spending his days playing music with Elvis and fishing and watching old movies."

I look down at my feet. Maybe he *was* doing those things, but now he's stuck here, back in the world that caused him so much pain, watching his family live and try to move on without him, because of me.

"He was a kind and loving man and"—she smiles— "brought kind and loving children into this world. And I know he would be so proud of you both."

As she smiles, tears brimming in her eyes, there's a shimmer in the air behind her left shoulder and a figure appears. He's nodding and smiling, and I can't help but smile back at them both. Maybe it wouldn't be so bad to have him here all the time, now that he's the man he always wanted to be. I'd have someone to talk to about movies and writing and maybe through me he could make music with Taylor and—

My mom's voice breaks into my thoughts. "He deserves to be at rest now."

Everyone in the circle nods and I bite my bottom lip, the vision I've created disintegrating. She's right. I look up and see that the light behind him is now barely the size of a coffee mug. He deserves rest, but he's running out of time and I still have no idea how to help him.

"Callie?" My mom is saying my name. She's already introduced me, but I didn't hear her. "Are you ready?"

I nod, though I'm not sure.

I step forward and lift my chin, looking around the circle. All I need to do is say a few nice things, right? I need to show him I remember good times, show my grandpa he wasn't all bad, prove to myself it wasn't *all* bad.

I look down at the list I created in my room last night.

"My dad liked to hum to himself, he was always thinking about music and spreading it through the world. Without him, without the humming, the world is a little quieter.

"He took up space in every room he entered. Not just physical space, because he was actually a pretty small guy, but he filled a room with his presence. Without him, every room is a little emptier."

Some people nod.

"He liked stories and he helped me become a storyteller. There was a bunny that lived under our shed behind the house and we named him Jacob Bunny. My dad helped us feed him and leave out carrots and lettuce and apples—he loved apples—and we kept an eye out for him every day.

My dad helped me write a story about a time I was scared our dog Bo had chased and killed Jacob, but it turned out Jacob had just gotten scared and hid under the shed and he soon came out looking for more apples."

I'm trying to focus on the memory, to clear my mind of the uncertainty and sadness of my child-hood, but when I see the shed where Jacob Bunny lived, I also see the day my cousin told me my dad was drunk, again, and I should tell my mom.

I shake my head and try another memory. "He also helped me write a story about a scary sound in the middle of the night that woke up a little girl but turned out to be the family cat stuck on the roof trying to get in through a window."

I hear Stormy banging on the loose screen in my bedroom window from the roof outside but behind that I hear a fist hitting a table and I almost jump.

I look up at him. He's smiling, but it's a polite smile and does not extend to his eyes. He is still here and the light behind him is getting smaller. This isn't working.

"He dressed up as a clown for my fifth birthday party. It was a little terrifying, honestly, but we all loved it."

I close my eyes and see the times we got to see him perform with his theater group, dressed up in wigs and thick makeup, and it didn't matter how good he was, I always wondered, *Has he been drinking?*

I try to focus on the last few days. Days I would have never had if he hadn't come back to make sure I was okay.

"He made the best spaghetti sauce."

I hear his sharp voice, *"Don't you ever think?"*

"And he loved movies and telling you every single fact he knew about that movie."

I see him stumbling toward me, asking me to dance.

"Everyone was his friend and he cared about strangers just as much as he cared about his friends and his family."

I see the man on the park bench and the life that might have been my dad's if it weren't for my mom.

"He made the best sandcastles and treated it like it was an art form, and when he did it, it was. Everything was art to him and he was really good at just about anything creative he put his mind to."

But he threw it all away. He never believed he was good enough and so he drank until it was true.

Why? Why did he throw it all away?

My mom is smiling and he's smiling, but he's still here and the light is still shrinking and I'm starting to panic. This isn't working.

I'm saying nice things and I even mean them, I mean them with all my heart, but I can't shake all of the other stuff. I can't talk about all the good without being haunted by the bad. My chest is tight and I'm suddenly having a hard time breathing.

"I'm sorry," I say, "I need a second."

I glance around, looking for somewhere, any-where to hide. There's not much in this wide-open field except a pole a few feet away, the remnants of an old fence. I step to the other side of the pole and lean against it. Everyone can still see me, but I can't see them, so it will have to do for the moment.

I hear my mom cover for me. "Taylor, why don't we play some music while we wait for Callie?"

Taylor must nod, because suddenly I hear the opening notes to one of his most popular songs; a few strums of a guitar, a pluck of a bass, a resounding trumpet and then, his deep baritone.

I half listen, half rack my brain for what I could do, what I could say to help him cross over.

I've spent quality time with him, I've let out my anger and yelled and apologized. There's nothing left to say, there's no answer, there's just a big gaping hole in my heart where my dad should be, filling it with movie quotes and life lessons and art and stories. Well, now he might be able to do all that, because if I don't think of something, he'll be stuck here. This is my last chance. My last chance to help him and I don't have any answers—to his questions or my own.

The trumpets sound again indicating a new verse and his voice fills my ears:

"If this be the last chance for us,

Don't stand asking why,

Let your voices ring together now,

And raise a final cry."

A sound escapes my throat as he launches into the chorus again—a laugh. I turn around to face the crowd. Some have their eyes closed and some are tapping their feet, but he is looking directly at me, waiting, his eyebrows lifted as if to say, *"That's what I was trying to tell you."*

The last notes of the song fade out along with his voice and I step back into the circle.

Everyone turns toward me, waiting.

I open my mouth and close it again.

He whispers, "I'm here, Callie. I'm listening."

This is it. He's here and ready to hear anything I have to say to him. I have a captive audience, people who would probably agree, or at least not blame me, if I chose to lay flat every grievance and let out all my anger right here and now. I could let it go. I could free myself and maybe him.

I open my mouth again and I am back to the day I first found him, desperate to speak but with words and a lifetime of feeling lodged in my throat.

Finally, my throat cracks and the words twist loose and I can speak.

"My dad did some terrible things in his lifetime." My mom winces, my grandpa nods, my dad drops his head. "He ate black licorice candy, for goodness' sake." A spattering of laughter from the circle. My mom tilts her head, waiting. "But he was still my dad. And he was so much more than his mistakes."

My mom smiles.

"He was an artist, a storyteller, a father, a friend, a movie lover, and a cook. He was funny, *sometimes*, and he was kind. In his heart of hearts, and even if it didn't always seem like it, he was selfless and would do anything for his family. He only wanted what was best for us and he did exactly what dads are supposed to do, he made sacrifices for his children. I know that now. Even if it took me a long time to see it. He only wanted the best for us, and that's all I want for him. I don't want him to hurt anymore.

"I thought I wanted answers," I continue. "I thought I needed to know *why* he did the things he did before I could truly accept him for who he was and begin to forgive him. But that's not fair. Forgiveness shouldn't have conditions. And sometimes, there just aren't any answers. Sometimes things aren't as simple as good or bad. Because my dad was all the things I just said and more, but he was also troubled, scared, and insecure. He was haunted by a past he didn't have the tools to face. And I understand that a little more now.

"I'm not making excuses for his behavior—he wouldn't want me to—but I'm also not going to let all the things he did cloud my perception of who he really *was*."

I let out a slow breath as I feel my bottom lip begin to quiver.

"I thought I wanted the chance to really let him have it." Some people in the audience chuckle. "I had a list of things I always thought I would say if my dad was ever standing in front of me again. But now I know, those things don't matter. All that matters is that after years of hurting, and running, and fighting, he gets to let go. He gets to rest.

Now I know I'll never get the answers I thought I needed and that's okay. Now I know exactly what I would say to him if he were standing in front of me again."

I take a deep breath. I lift my gaze to his, but tears cloud my vision and my voice cracks as I finally say the thing weighing most heavily on my heart.

"I miss you."

That's all. It's that simple. And that's what does it. As I watch, never breaking eye contact with the man watching me with a wide smile and a bottom lip quivering just as much as mine, he begins to fade.

My mom reaches over and grabs my hand and whispers, "I miss him, too."

My brother nods next to me and bumps my shoulder with his. "Me, too."

And soon everyone around me is nodding and mumbling everything they miss about him, their voices ringing together. No one is talking about his drinking, just his laugh and his music and his generous heart. No one is asking why, and he isn't ashamed. He isn't hiding or trying to disappear, but he is fading. The light behind him that only seconds ago had shrunk down to the size of a pin-prick is growing bigger and brighter and enveloping him and showing through him. His jet-black hair looks like someone has taken an eraser to it and his eyes are shining. I hold eye contact for as long as possible, and just before a bright explosion of light, I hear a whisper on the wind. "I love you, Callie. Thank you."

*Listen to "Run
For Your
Brother," by
Eddie Spooner*

Two Months Later

I'm watching the horizon, oh my God, what do I see? Are there angels in the heavens, looking down on me?

E.S.

*W*hen my dad died, I was sad.
When he came back, I was pissed.

I pause and look up sheepishly from the words I am reading on the paper clutched in my hands.

"Those were the first lines of the story I turned in. And before you get all hurt, *you* told me to tell the truth. And I got an A."

I look back down at the paper and there, under the "A," are the words, *Now that's emotion.*

"I think my professor realized it was a little more nonfiction than one would normally find in a fiction class, but he assumed the ghost part was fake and so he let it slide."

I roll my eyes up at the blue sky.

"It was a little more nonfiction than I would have liked it to be too, but . . ." I shrug and lie back on the blanket I've spread out in the grass. Harley brought me a pitcher of iced tea, like she often did when she saw my car pull up to the field, patted my shoulder, and then left me to my visit. She'd told me to stop parking at the bottom of the drive a few trips back, that I was welcome to come visit her or the field any day and I didn't have to worry about disturbing her.

"He's definitely not here anymore," she told me on one of my early visits, "but something dances in that field on the days you visit."

Nothing is dancing today. The mid-May sun is unseasonably hot and there is no breeze to move the grass or cool my skin. I won't be staying long. Taylor said he would help unload my car and move me into my old room for the summer and I couldn't keep him from his busy social life.

It will be quiet at home this summer, peaceful. A whole year separating us from the shock of the loss, my first summer in this new space I'm in. I have to admit, despite the emptiness that creeps in when I really focus on his absence, I'm looking forward to that peace.

But I'd wanted to make sure he knew about the story he'd played such a large part in writing, and my final grade.

"I guess I should be thanking you for my passing grade. The story of a girl who has to face her feelings for her dead alcoholic father through a journey of acceptance and growth is just the kind of thing writing professors *love*." I sigh. "So . . . thanks."

Words aren't hard to find anymore when I come to the field. Whether it's Harley's presence and her connection to the other world, or my acceptance of my dad—the good, the bad, and the complicated—I feel him here with me every time I visit. And when I feel him next to me or above me or wherever he is,

I know there is no use holding back. He needs me to tell him about our lives and remember him when we go about living them, and as much as I've never wanted to admit it, I need him. I need my dad.

It doesn't mean I'm not mad at him.

I need him and he's not here and that *does* piss me off.

I miss him and I will always have to miss him and that's not fair.

I sigh and close my eyes against fresh tears. Crying comes a little more easily these days too. All the tears I'd held back for so long finally making their way out, I suppose.

I try to keep talking.

"He told me I should enter it in a contest, that it stood a chance at winning. And he said that if this was a topic I was 'familiar' with, I should keep writing about it, that there are probably a lot of people who need to hear what I want to say." I turn onto my side, my back already sweating. "I guess if you were here, I wouldn't have anything to write about." I sigh. "But that doesn't mean you're forgiven!"

Forgiveness would take time.

Tears slide down my cheeks with my shift in position and I sit up and wipe them away.

"Well, I suppose I should-"

Before I can stand, a breeze comes out of nowhere and rustles the grass and weeds surrounding me—a breeze that has no business blowing on a day like this. It cools my cheeks like a gentle kiss, and on the wind, like a lullaby, a sweet song on a sleepless night, I hear, *"Dance with me."*

I freeze, an almost automatic answer of "no" pausing on my tongue. I look from the ground to the sky, two scenarios playing through my head like a movie.

I could sit here, stewing in my sadness and sweat, longing for the things I cannot change. I could go home, feeling sad and alone and a little sorry for myself, and try to avoid the past as I forge a new beginning.

Or, I could show him I'm okay. That he'd taught me to enjoy small moments like building sandcastles on a warm spring day, to take the time to help strangers, and to accept the things I cannot change instead of hiding from them. I could drop the boulders of resentment that still sometimes make their way onto my shoulders, even if only for a few moments, and frolic my way around this field, my right hand clasping an invisible one and my left resting on an imaginary shoulder. I could take two minutes to show my dad that even though he's put our family through hell, he's still my dad and I love him.

I *should* dance.

I stand up from the blanket.

I can picture his thin hand reaching out to clasp mine and his short torso straightening as he readies himself for the movement. I see his eyes twinkling in the afternoon sunlight, clear and completely focused on me.

I look up to the sky, letting go of guilt and anger and brushing away tears and demons.

"Sing me a song, and I will."

And so, we dance.

The End

(and a beginning)

Afterword

My father died 24 years ago and if he came back today, if the events depicted in this book actually happened, I would still be mad.

I would still be conflicted at the sight of him rather than relieved to see him again. Sure, I understand addiction a little better today than I did as a teenager, I know it's a disease and that the actions of the addict aren't always their fault. But if I saw him again today, I would still be mad about everything he put us through, mad he never got better, and mad that he left us. And that's ok.

I hope this book shows everyone that has lost someone to addiction, whether through death or simply because they are no longer the person they once were, that you can miss them, be sad they're gone, and mourn their loss...and still be mad.

You might always be mad. You might always be conflicted. You might always be afraid you're a terrible person because you're relieved they're gone...you're not. You may always find yourself waiting for the day you feel at peace about the loss, feel the burden lift off your shoulders and suddenly find forgiveness...you might not.

We may always be mad, but the only thing we can do to find a little peace is to realize that all those feelings are okay, that the conflict and anger and confusion are justified, and that all we can do is accept the things we cannot change, find courage to change the things we can, and, hopefully, the wisdom to know the difference. [1]

---

1. The Serenity Prayer

Thank Yous

The people who helped make this book a reality know who they are. I was able to thank some of the most important people in my life in my last book so I won't repeat those sentiments here, but you all are my tribe and I will be forever grateful for each and every one of you.

This book would not exist without those people but it also would not exist without a few specific communities.

To my fellow artists, whether you are writers, poets, musicians, painters, or dancers; you are everything that is beautiful in this world. My dad knew the importance of art and it is only because of you, the community of artists I see hard at work every day, that I was able to find the courage to write this book. Your bravery made me brave. Your vulnerability made it easier for me to be vulnerable. Your talent inspired me to dig deep and push the limits of my art with every new piece. Thank you for creating, thank you for making the world a brighter place. And to the community of artists in *my* community—thank you for your heART.

To my early readers and my BookTok community; your words, your encouragement, your love of reading and your determination to support Indie Authors, humbles me. Thank you for your support and your passion.

And if you found yourself in the pages of this book, whether in the words or you were just there during this part of my life, thank you for being a part of my journey.

And to my brother; thank you for helping me capture his voice and for continuing his legacy through your talent, your kindness, and your gentle spirit. I know he would be so very proud of the man you have become.

About the author

Allison Spooner is the author of the Amazon Bestseller and #1 New Release, *The Lost Girl: A Neverland Story*. She's also published two collections of genre-crossing flash fiction, *Flash in the Dark: A Collection of Flash Fiction* and *The Problem with Humans: And Other Stories*, and has contributed to several horror and science fiction anthologies.

Her stories have been called, "unique works of art," and "brilliant, disturbing, and thought-provoking," and The Lost Girl was the winner of the 2024 PenCraft Seasonal Book Award Winter

Competition. When she isn't writing, Allison loves reading, doing yoga, trying not to kill her plants, encouraging other writers over on TikTok, and spending time with her family in her home state of Michigan. You can learn more about her or connect on allisonspoonerwriter.com.

P.S. If you enjoyed this book, PLEASE go leave a review on your favorite platform. Reviews mean the world to Indie Authors and can help get their books seen by more people.

www.ingramcontent.com/pod-product-compliance
Lightning Source LLC
Chambersburg PA
CBHW011410310726
48972CB00011B/2923